MW01100597

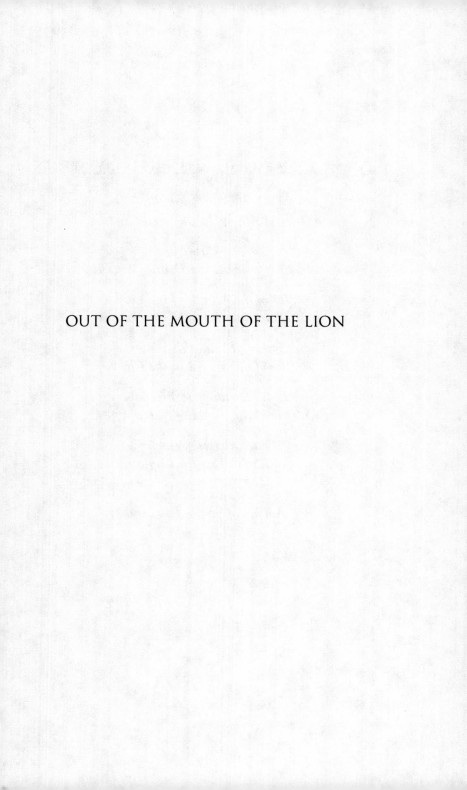

OUT OF THE MOUTH OF THE LION

Emma Leslie Church History Series

THE CHURCH IN THE CATACOMBS

Page 25

EMMA LESLIE CHURCH HISTORY SERIES

OUT OF THE MOUTH OF THE LION

OR

THE CHURCH IN THE CATACOMBS

BY

EMMA LESLIE

Illustrated by
FELTER, GUNSTON, BUTTERWORTH & HEATH

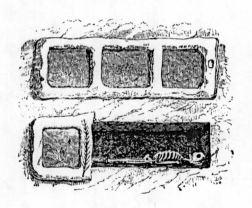

Salem Ridge Press
Emmaus, Pennsylvania

Originally Published
1875
The Religious Tract Society

Republished 2007
Salem Ridge Press LLC
4263 Salem Drive
Emmaus, Pennsylvania 18049

www.salemridgepress.com

Hardcover ISBN: 978-1-934671-04-7
Softcover   ISBN: 978-1-934671-05-4

PUBLISHER'S NOTE

In *Out of the Mouth of the Lion* Emma Leslie brings
to life the Seven Churches of Revelation and uses
their commitment, or lack thereof, to remind us
that when persecution comes, every Christian has
a choice to make. From the fictional Flavia who
remains faithful to Christ despite the threat of
losing everything she loves, to Polycarp, Bishop
of Smyrna, an early martyr and hero of the faith,
we are challenged by a devotion to God that nothing in this world can shake.

Commitment to God cannot be built in a day.
It is the result of conscious, daily decisions to live
for God no matter what the cost. When Polycarp
was told to deny God or die he boldly answered,
"Fourscore and six years have I been His servant,
and He hath done me no wrong. How then can
I blaspheme my King who saved me?" God has
been faithful to us and my prayer is that through
this book each of us will be inspired to commit
our lives each day to His service.

Daniel Mills

November, 2007

PREFACE TO 1875 EDITION

In my former story, *Glaucia*, I attempted to give
some idea of the difficulties with which Christianity had to contend, in the manners, customs, and
modes of thought of the age in which it was intro-
duced.

In the present volume I have taken my readers
forward a hundred years—years in which the Gospel had made such rapid strides that from the bor-
ders of China and the plains of India to the shores
of Germany and of Britain Christian churches had
been planted; and, in not a few of them, faithful
men had sealed their testimony with their blood.

Various causes had combined to bring about
this wonderful result. Many of the Roman legionaries had learned to serve Christ as well as the emperor, and had carried with them to the remotest
provinces of the empire the glad tidings that there
was a God and Saviour, even for the poor and oppressed. The character of the converts deepened
the impression made by the message of the Gospel. Their courage, steadfastness, holiness, and
serene hopefulness could not be without effect in
an age of licentiousness, restlessness, and despair.
"See how these Christians love one another!" was
the admiring confession wrung from the lips even
of their enemies. And as the ennobling principles

LEGIONARIES: *Roman soldiers*
LICENTIOUSNESS: *no moral restraint*

taught by Christ and His apostles became better understood, not a few who had sought peace in the study of philosophy turned wearily from the vain pursuit to find rest for their souls in "the truth as it is in Jesus."

Surprise has sometimes been expressed that under the ample religious toleration of the Roman empire Christians should have suffered persecution. The mythologies of the conquered world had been absorbed and adopted by the conquerors. The deities of Egypt, Persia, and Syria had their temples and votaries in the Imperial city. The Pantheon was a public recognition of this fact. Why then should Christianity alone be singled out for ruthless extirpation? The answer is to be found in its aggressive and exclusive character. It denounced idolatry in every form. It declared that the heathen worshiped devils and not God. To burn incense to the statue of the emperor, to acknowledge him as *pontifex maximus*, to join in those religious ceremonies which formed part of the political system of the State would be treachery to its Divine King and Lord. Christianity might have been recognised as a *religio licita*, if it could have stooped to take its place amongst the other tolerated creeds. But this it could not do. Hence the universal hatred with which it was regarded, the pitiless persecution with which it was assailed.

In selecting the reign of Marcus Aurelius as the

VOTARIES: *worshipers*
EXTIRPATION: *destruction*
PONTIFEX MAXIMUS: *high priest, literally "the greatest bridge-builder" in Latin*

PREFACE

date of my second story, I have purposely avoided the sickening and heart-rending tragedies enacted under the Domitian, Decian, and Diocletian persecutions. Under the mild and gentle Marcus Aurelius the prefects of the different provinces were doubtless more to blame than the emperor, and these were urged—often driven—to their cruel work by the infuriated mobs who echoed the words and threats of the priests of Jupiter.

I have endeavoured, in the details of the following narrative, to adhere as closely as possible to the facts of history. Those of my readers who may wish to acquaint themselves more fully with the scenes amid which a large part of the story is laid—the Seven Churches of Asia—are referred to Canon Tristram's able and learned work, *The Seven Golden Candlesticks*. Lest it should be thought that in the description of the martyrdom of Polycarp I have painted the soldiers as too cruel even for those days, I may mention that in the contemporary account of his arrest it is stated that two children of the village were seized, and being asked where the aged bishop was living, one was beaten to death rather than betray his hiding-place. The other revealed it under similar torture.

That we in these days may learn a lesson of steadfast patience and gentle firmness from the contemplation of these faithful witnesses for Christ is the prayer of—

The Author

RELIGIO LICITA: *tolerated religion*
CREEDS: *sets of beliefs*

HISTORICAL NOTES

The early Christians faced persecution from the Roman government at various times beginning with Nero in A.D. 64. At the time when *Out of the Mouth of the Lion* takes place, A.D. 161-166, Christianity was illegal in the Roman Empire but most of the persecution was stirred up by angry mobs rather than being official persecution.

Several important historical figures from the second century A.D. are mentioned in *Out of the Mouth of the Lion*. Here is a brief summary of three of these people:

Marcus Aurelius: Marcus Aurelius, Emperor of Rome from A.D. 161-180, was born in A.D. 121. In A.D. 138 he was adopted by future emperor Antoninus Pius and seven years later married Faustina, daughter of Antoninus Pius who was now Emperor. Together Marcus Aurelius and Faustina had thirteen children, six daughters and seven sons. Following the death of Emperor Antoninus Pius, Marcus Aurelius became Emperor, reigning for nearly twenty years until his death. Marcus Aurelius was a lifelong student of Stoic philosophy and wrote a book, called *Meditations*, on his beliefs about life.

HISTORICAL NOTES

Polycarp: As a young man Polycarp was trained in the Christian faith by the Apostle John and other apostles. Appointed the Bishop of Smyrna, Polycarp was a respected teacher who helped to determine the reliability and authenticity of the many letters circulating among the churches. His long life and martyrdom were a great inspiration to the growing church.

Melito: Melito, Bishop of Sardis, was an important defender of Christianity during the second century A.D. He wrote extensively, including a defense of the Christian faith that was sent to Emperor Marcus Aurelius. He was also one of the first Christians to attempt to compile the Old Testament Scriptures. Melito died in A.D. 180 of natural causes and was buried at Sardis.

IMPORTANT DATES

A.D.

96 The Apostle John writes *Revelation* on the Isle of Patmos

97 The Apostle John returns to Ephesus from exile

139 Justin Martyr writes his *First Apology* for the Christians

161 Marcus Aurelius becomes Emperor of Rome

166 Martyrdom of Polycarp

180 Death of Marcus Aurelius

REVELATION 1:10-20, 3:22

"I was in the Spirit on the Lord's day, and heard behind me a great voice, as of a trumpet, Saying, 'I am Alpha and Omega, the first and the last: and, What thou seest, write in a book, and send it unto the seven churches which are in Asia; unto **Ephesus**, *and unto* **Smyrna**, *and unto* **Pergamos**, *and unto* **Thyatira**, *and unto* **Sardis**, *and unto* **Philadelphia**, *and unto* **Laodicea**.'*

"And I turned to see the voice that spake with me. And being turned, I saw seven golden candlesticks; And in the midst of the seven candlesticks one like unto the Son of man, clothed with a garment down to the foot, and girt about the paps with a golden girdle. His head and his hairs were white like wool, as white as snow; and his eyes were as a flame of fire; And his feet like unto fine brass, as if they burned in a furnace; and his voice as the sound of many waters. And he had in his right hand seven stars: and out of his mouth went a sharp twoedged sword: and his countenance was as the sun shineth in his strength. And when I saw him, I fell at his feet as dead. And he laid his right hand upon me, saying unto me, 'Fear not; I am the first and the last: I am he that liveth, and was dead; and, behold, I am alive for evermore, Amen; and have the keys of hell and of death. Write the things which thou hast seen, and the things which are, and the things which shall be hereafter; The mystery of the seven stars which thou sawest in my right hand, and the seven golden candlesticks. The seven stars are the angels of the seven churches: and the seven candlesticks which thou sawest are the seven churches...

"'...He that hath an ear, let him hear what the Spirit saith unto the churches.'"

THE SEVEN CHURCHES
OF REVELATON

Thracia
(Modern-day Turkey)

Black Sea

Sea of Marmara

Pergamos

Thyatira

Sardis

Smyrna

Philadelphia

Ephesus

Laodicea

Asia Minor
(Modern-day Turkey)

Ægean Sea

Miles

0   50   100

Mediterranean Sea

·····>······> Path of Flaminius and his family

CONTENTS

ILLUSTRATIONS

OUT OF THE MOUTH OF THE LION

OUT OF THE MOUTH OF THE LION

CHAPTER I

THE MIDNIGHT MEETING

 HE sun was slowly sinking behind the Alban hills, and the shadows were growing longer and longer in the lovely valley of Aricia, while upon the forests of evergreen oaks and cork-trees that clothed the lower slopes of the mountains, night had already descended. But in spite of the lengthening shadows and deepening gloom there was an unusual stir and bustle. Instead of retiring

to their homes, all the inhabitants of the valley seemed to be going out in holiday attire with baskets and bundles, in which one could catch glimpses of goats'-milk cheese, dried dates and figs, as well as cakes and barley bread.

Gay equipages, preceded by slaves, were also to be seen mingling with the more humble holiday-makers, and they all took the same road across the Campagna towards the gate of the Imperial City. Men and women, with children in their arms or at their side; patrician ladies, who would not soil their feet by stepping across the streets where the poorer citizens walked, were all talking of the same subject this evening, all bent on the same errand—to reach the Flavian Amphitheater tonight, that they might secure seats to witness the games; for although that mighty edifice, now known as the Colosseum, would accommodate eighty thousand spectators, hundreds would struggle in vain to reach its marble seats, and would go away at last disappointed.

"Mother, will the lion be very fierce?" asked a gentle-looking, fair-haired girl, vainly trying to suppress a shudder as she spoke.

"Julia is afraid of the lion, I know," said her brother. "He cannot come to us, silly girl," he added; "it's only those wicked Christians that the lion can touch."

"Come, come, children!" called the father at this moment. "We must make haste, or the city

GAY: *brightly-colored*
EQUIPAGES: *horse-drawn carriages*
CAMPAGNA: *a residential area surrounding Rome*

gates will be closed, and then we shall see nothing of the games tomorrow."

A litter, in which sat two ladies, was traveling in the same direction, and at about the same pace, as the vinedresser's family, and the children's talk about the next day's grand doings seemed to interest and amuse them very much.

"I wonder whether we were as eager to see the shows as these children are when we first went," said Flavia, the elder of the two sisters.

"Yes, indeed," answered her sister, gaily; "and I am anxious to see the closing scene of this spectacle. Chariot riding and gladiators fighting are sights common enough; but the king of beasts fighting with half a dozen Christians is a sight Rome has not witnessed for several years."

"No, I have never seen them in the arena," said her sister. "The law of Trajan, that these people should be punished only when they broke the laws of Rome, has prevented the prefects from yielding to the wish of the people when they demanded that they should be thrown to the lions for worshiping strange gods," replied Flavia.

"Well, it does not seem quite fair that these people should be so severely punished for not worshiping the gods of Rome. Serapis, for whom our late emperor erected such a splendid temple, is not a Roman god, and yet he is honoured here as in Egypt. Indeed, it is quite fashionable to worship both Serapis and Isis in Rome."

PATRICIAN: *the upper class in ancient Rome*
PREFECTS: *high Roman officials*
SERAPIS AND ISIS: *Egyptian gods*

"Nay, nay, Sisidona! It is not for the worship of this God alone, but the manner of their worship, that makes everyone hate them so much. We love our Eleusinian mysteries, it is true, but the orgies of these vile Christians are far, far worse than anything ever heard of before. Children are decoyed into these meetings, and never heard of or seen afterwards."

Sisidona shuddered. "To think of sweet little innocents, like thy Flaminia, being ill-used," she said. "I would have every one of them thrown to the lions or into the Tiber," she added, quickly.

The young matron smiled at her sister's earnestness. "There is little fear that thou wilt turn Christian."

"The gods forbid any Roman matron or maiden joining this accursed sect. What thinkest thou, Flaminius?" she added, lifting the curtain of her litter and addressing a young man in the chariot at the side. "Flavia deems it needful to give me a word of warning concerning these wretched Christians."

"Hush, hush, my sister," said the young man, with a smile. "Jest not about this, for strangers who know thee not may suspect that thou needest the caution, and this would bring trouble upon all of us;" and he glanced at the gentleman beside him as he spoke.

Sisidona pouted like a spoiled child. "My friends need not trouble themselves about me," she said;

ELEUSINIAN MYSTERIES: *religious secrets associated with the worship of the Greek gods, Demeter and Persephone*
ORGIES: *wild rituals*

but she, too, glanced at the other occupant of the chariot as she spoke.

"The noble Sisidona will never cause her friends anxiety on that account, I am sure," he said, in answer to her look.

"I never make any promises," said the young lady, archly.

"Then my Flavia must take charge of her willful little sister," said Flaminius, with a loving look at his wife as he spoke.

"She will not prove a troublesome charge. But shall we not be late?" said the lady, hastily, noticing for the first time the deepening shadows along the road.

"Yes, we must not linger talking here, or we shall have to stay outside the city gates until the morning;" and the next minute slaves and horses were urged to a brisker pace, and they hurried across the Campagna, for they were anxious to secure lodgings in the already crowded city, and this would not be easy, they knew, on the eve of such a splendid exhibition in the arena.

Meanwhile the streets of the city were thronged with eager sightseers, all on their way to or from the Colosseum; for those whom business would prevent, as well as many who did not intend venturing to be present the following day, were determined to see something of the spectacle, and went to see the lion confined in its cage at the side of the building; while those

ARCHLY: *impudently*

who hoped to occupy one of those marble seats now shining dim and white in the fading daylight were eagerly pressing toward the different entrances, where a dense crowd had already assembled.

These were variously engaged in betting on the gladiators, and talking over the additional spectacle of the lion and the Christians, some wishing the emperor had ordered them to be armed, that the unequal contest might be prolonged, and others that they might be brought out one at the time. But no one ventured to breathe a word of pity for those who were condemned to this awful punishment, even if they felt any compassion.

The crowd consisted of the poorer classes, wool-carders and dyers, tanners, and the miners or excavators who dug the stone, of which Rome was built, from the interior of the adjacent hills. These far outnumbered the other portion; and when it became known in which of the numerous cells that intersected the lower portion of the great amphitheater the prisoners were confined, several of these rough-looking men left the doorway, near which they were standing, and made their way to the deserted side of the vast building. After cautiously looking round to see that no one was within earshot, they went to one of the thickly-studded, grated doors, and one said in a loud whisper, "Courage, my brethren and sister, the Lord will be near ye."

IMPERIAL PURPLE: *certain shades of purple could only be worn by the Roman Emperor*

"Yes, nearer than the crowd or the lion, for He is with us now, brightening this dark cell with the glory of His presence," said a firm cheerful voice from within.

"The Lord be praised!" said the visitors, and then gathered closer to the door that they might hear every word spoken, while one went to tell other friends that they had succeeded in finding the prison.

As the shades of night grew more dark the crowds in the streets leading to the Colosseum increased both in noise and number; and whatever other topic they might disagree upon, all joined in praise of their new emperor, Marcus Aurelius, who, at the festivities on his assumption of the imperial purple, promised to gratify his people's wish, and put down these Christians. So eager, so intent was everybody in the discussion of this and kindred topics, that no one noticed a little group of quiet-speaking, unostentatious people, who pushed their way through the crowd when compelled to do it, but otherwise sought the shelter of walls and porticoes as they pressed on toward the center of attraction, the Colosseum.

It was reached at last, but they did not turn toward the spot where the fierce roaring of the lion gave notice of where he was to be seen, but passed on toward another cell, from whence other sounds than this were now heard. The little group of Christians, outside as well as inside the cell, had

UNOSTENTATIOUS: *not showy*
PORTICOES: *covered entrance areas or porches where the roof is supported by pillars*

lifted their voices in concert, and were singing a hymn. Softly and sweetly came the muffled sound from within the iron grating; but the fresh-comers heard it before they reached the spot, and joined in the strain that told of life beyond the grave. Victor, their bishop, was with the little party outside. When the singing had ceased he went close to the door, and, though the grating was high above his head, he made himself heard while he spoke words of faith and hope to brace the courage of those about to suffer. If the glory and honour of martyrdom was pictured in such glowing language that those standing without almost envied their comrades within those stone walls, was it greatly to be wondered at? It was no common trial they were called upon to endure. The hisses and scornful words of thousands of spectators were in themselves enough to make the stoutest heart quail, and these, as well as the lion, would have to be confronted in a few hours.

When Victor had done speaking another hymn was sung, and then the bishop again drew near the door, and, with upraised head and outstretched arms, he prayed for those so soon to suffer an agonizing death; prayed that the Lord Himself would stand by them, as He did by His servant Daniel, either to shut the lion's mouth, or to grant them a speedy deliverance from the agonies of death, and an abundant entrance into the kingdom of light. But not only for those, or the Church of God in

Rome, did he pray but for that clamouring, quarrelsome multitude, whose shouting and struggling could be heard now, and who, scarcely less savage than the lion himself, had thirsted for their blood, and demanded it of the emperor. For those he prayed, that they might be turned from the worship of demons to the living God; that some of those who should assemble to witness the death of these Christians might be so impressed that they, too, should become seekers after God.

The deep blue of the midnight sky, with its myriad stars, saw the little company of Christians increase in number as well as in fervour. All fear of what the consequences might be had vanished, and many, as they joined in singing the soul-cheering words of their hymns, wished they could change places with their companions in the cell, or that someone would accuse them of holding the same faith, that they, too, might march to the arena the next day. The fear of death was taken away, and those whom a few in the distant crowd silently pitied as the most miserable people in Rome, were exulting in the anticipation of the glory so soon to be revealed. Those to be cheered and comforted had changed places before the little company broke up, for it was those within the cell who were speaking words of hope and joy and encouragement, while many outside were bowed down with grief and sorrow, and dared not trust their voices to respond for fear of betraying their emotion.

MYRIAD: *countless*
EXULTING: *rejoicing*

At length, however, the last words had to be spoken—messages sent to absent friends from those within the cells, last wishes expressed, and then the last farewell. They could not see each other face to face—that joy could not be theirs until they met before the throne of God—but words of tenderest love and affection were uttered, and then, as the first rosy flush of dawn began to paint the eastern sky, the little company turned sorrowfully away, and silently took the road leading to their homes. A few of the boldest of them would fain have mingled with the crowd now pressing round the entrances, that they might by their presence, cheer and encourage their companions when they should be brought forth; but this their bishop deemed unwise in the present instance, and so, for the sake of others, these restrained their eagerness, and went back to their daily employment of wool-combing, or cutting out blocks of stone, and thus forming those wonderful cells and passages since known as the Catacombs. These cells the poor of Rome had been glad to use as sepulchers, for they could not afford to burn their dead, as the wealthy and patrician families did. Another use had now been found for some of the large chambers, for here the Christian Church could meet without fear of interruption or discovery, for none save the *fossors*, or those working in the catacombs, understood the tortuous windings of these subterranean passages, and it was among

FAIN: *gladly*
SEPULCHERS: *tombs*
TORTUOUS: *twisting*

these poor and despised workmen that the Gospel made its way most rapidly, so that the secret was comparatively safe from the rest of the world.

To this underground church many of the Christians now took their way, and while trumpets were blowing, and flags were being unfurled, and chariots driving at their topmost speed, and all fashionable Rome turning out to witness the grand scene of the day, they were praying for their companions, that their faith and courage might not fail, and for the emperor and his people, that they, too, might learn to seek God.

CHAPTER II

AT THE COLOSSEUM

WHATEVER rest Rome had enjoyed the night before the shows in the arena, it was broken at the earliest dawn of day, for all who desired to witness them must present their tickets at the various entrances early if they wished to obtain a seat; and so before the first rays of the sun had gilded the colossal statue of Apollo, standing in the midst of the Triumphal Way, the broad street was crowded with silk-curtained litters, and gay, fantastic chariots, surrounded by their slaves, whose efforts were, however, of no avail in clearing a passage through such a dense crowd, although they used their rods upon the unfortunate foot-passengers who happened to be in the way.

Just beyond the colossal statue of the sun god rose the vast Flavian Amphitheater, its marble seats rising tier above tier, the most conspicuous in the lower one being reserved for the emperor and his household and the senators. Behind these sat the magistrates and wealthy patricians, and

FANTASTIC: *extravagant*

then the male portion of the general public. The upper seats were exclusively set apart for women; and now, in the morning sunshine, their gay dresses looked as bright as a parterre of flowers; and here there was more laughing, betting, and joking than in any of the other seats. Around the parapet, which was raised above the arena, and from which the seats gradually rose, were gladiatorial inscriptions, while the arena itself was covered with fine sifted sand.

It was not long when the doors were once opened before the whole building was filled, and every eye was directed to the silk-curtained ivory box, where Marcus Aurelius would take his place as emperor today for the first time. It would not be the first time he had sat near the imperial chair, for he had not only been the adopted heir, but the loved and trusted friend of his predecessor, Antoninus Pius, and none mourned his death more deeply and truly than the man who was to succeed to his honours, and all Rome knew it.

At last a flourish of trumpets announced the arrival of the emperor, and every eye was strained to catch a glimpse of that noble brow and calmly beautiful, though somewhat sad face. As if divining this wish, he stood for a moment and gazed round upon that immense multitude, now rending the air with their shouts, and chatted with his coadjutor, Lucius Verus, and an old Roman general, Avidius Cassius, who stood near. Then sitting

PARTERRE: *ornamental garden*
PREDECESSOR: *the one who held the position before him*
COADJUTOR: *assistant*

down, he motioned to a young man, who carried a roll of manuscript, to come close to his chair and prepare to commence reading. He himself at the same time drew from his girdle the waxen tablets and stylus, to take notes of anything that should take place worthy of being remembered. As soon as the emperor had taken his seat the trumpets again sounded. The next minute the gladiators entered the arena, and, forming into a procession, marched slowly round the vast space, stopping in front of the emperor's seat as they shouted, "Hail, Cæsar! those about to die salute thee."

It was the usual form of salutation; but how surprised some of that gay, thoughtless multitude would have been, could they have known what their great Cæsar was writing as he bent over his tablets when the gladiators turned away. Slowly the clumsy golden pen formed the words: "It would be a man's happiest lot to depart from mankind without having had a taste of lying, and hypocrisy, and luxury, and pride. However, to breathe out one's life when a man has had enough of those things is the next best voyage."

Strange words these for such a man to write; for Marcus Aurelius was no common man, but a king among his fellows by nature as well as by circumstance. A Roman, a patrician, in the full tide of health, of glorious beauty, the greatest philosopher, the noblest ruler of his time, master of the world, and yet he could see the hollowness and

GIRDLE: *belt*

vanity of it all; and instead of being sunk in luxury or intoxicated with the vast power he possessed, could yet aspire and long for something purer, holier, nobler than any life that could be lived here. Surely the Spirit of God implanted these holy aspirations and longings after greater purity and truth, although he knew it not. Surely God was waiting to reveal Himself more clearly to this, the noblest of Rome's emperors. But will Marcus Aurelius see Him for whom he is stretching out weary hands blindly, if haply he may find Him? Will he recognize His humble messengers, or will he persecute those to whom he is nearest in aim and spirit?

By the time the emperor had finished writing in his tablets the first preliminaries of the games were over, and the sham contest between the gladiators began. Fighting with wooden swords, however, was too tame for a Roman populace, and was speedily brought to a close. The real gladiatorial games now began, and they paired off and assumed the different weapons they were to use. The first gladiator carried a net and spear, while his opponent bore shield and sword, and this was considered one of the most artistic portions of the games. The next couple were Greeks, naked save a cincture round the waist. These were each armed with a heavy cestus. Another pair followed in complete armour of steel, and armed with sharp-pointed swords.

HAPLY: *by accident*
CINCTURE: *belt*
CESTUS: *a leather glove weighted with iron or lead*

It was no sham fighting now. The sand and sawdust covering the arena were soon soaked with blood, and the multitude shouted and cheered first one combatant and then another, until the netter fell dead beneath a blow from his opponent's sword, when a shout for the victor announced that the first contest was over.

The attendants came in with hooks and fresh sand, and dragging away the body of the gladiator to the *spoliarium*, the arena was sprinkled with the sand, and another pair stepped forward to fight until one or other should drop beneath a fatal blow, and be dragged off, as their companion had been. Horrible as the sight was, hundreds of Rome's proudest and fairest patrician dames sat and watched each detail, while children clapped their tiny hands at the sight of the blood-stained corpses.

The emperor alone seemed to take little interest in the spectacle. His position obliged him to be present, but he paid far more heed to the reading than to the pageant. And what was the book, and who was the author that could interest such a man as Marcus Aurelius, and at such a time as this? The book was called "The Discourses of Epictetus," and he was a Phrygian slave; but the emperor was nonetheless glad to learn from him. How strange it would have sounded to some of those frivolous Romans to hear these words read from this book: "Nothing great is produced at once; the

NETTER: *a gladiator fighting with a net*
SPOLIARIUM: *a pit where the dead gladiators were dragged*
PHRYGIAN: *someone from Phrygia, in modern-day Turkey*

vine must blossom, and bear fruit, and ripen, before we have the purple clusters of the grape....But how are we to know that we have made progress? We may know it if our own wills are bent in conformity with nature; if we be noble, free, faithful, humble; if desiring nothing and shunning nothing which lies beyond our power we sit loose to all earthly interests; if our lives are under the distinct governance of immutable and noble laws."

These were the words Marcus Aurelius was pondering, as he sat in the chair of state, gazed at and envied by that mighty crowd. While these gladiators fought with sword and cestus the emperor was thinking how he could best fight against his own selfishness and the first rising of misplaced ambition; how he might train himself to become a better ruler, and a nobler, purer man; and the best help, the best guidance he could have, that he knew of, were the words of this Phrygian slave. He had perhaps never heard of the Bible, never heard of God's Holy Spirit, who has promised to be not only the Comforter, but the Guide and Helper of all who seek Him; and so it was no wonder that the emperor sighed as he thought how hard the battle was to fight. And yet, although he knew it not, surely God's Spirit was his Helper, or he could never have lived such a pure, noble, unselfish life in the midst of people so corrupt and vicious that all virtue seemed dead, so sunk in luxury and selfish indulgence that they would sell themselves to

IMMUTABLE: *unchangeable*

the most abject slavery to secure it. The grand old Roman virtues had passed away, and Rome had fallen a victim to her universal conquest, being herself conquered by the vices of her tributary provinces, so that she had become an aggregate of vice and depravity. Yet in the midst of all this, her emperor was struggling nobly against evil propensities in himself, and doing what he could to encourage virtue, goodness, and truth in others, but still groping in the darkness, not knowing that the Light had come, and was even now shining in the hearts of many whom he had been taught to consider the vilest of his subjects.

The gladiatorial contests came to an end at last. The gory corpses were dragged away, fresh sand and sawdust were sprinkled on the floor of the arena, and people shook out their dresses and settled themselves comfortably in their seats for the last grand scene that was yet to be enacted. The emperor, however, rose and left the Colosseum at this point, and his seat was taken by the prefect who had condemned the Christians to the lions on the very day Marcus Aurelius was proclaimed emperor.

Meanwhile the little company of believers in their gloomy cell were alternately praying for strength to be faithful to their Lord, and encouraging each other by repeating portions of Scripture they had learned. Once or twice they ventured to sing a hymn, and they were thus engaged when the

ABJECT: *miserable, wretched*
VICES: *sinful practices*
TRIBUTARY PROVINCES: *provinces that pay tribute*

door swung gratingly back, and disclosed that sea
of faces rising up before them. For a moment they
were dazzled by the sudden burst of sunshine, and
Melita, who had followed her husband and father
to prison and to death, uttered a slight scream. Her
husband looked pityingly at the white, frightened
face of his wife, and putting his arm around her,
whispered, "Courage, my Melita; close thine eyes
and lean on me; the Lord Christ will bear thee in
His arms to the glory beyond."

The white-headed old man who was to suffer
too, stepped out first, marched with a firm step
to the middle of the arena, and turned his face
toward the prefect. Melita's fright on seeing so
many faces turned toward her soon passed away.
Leaning on her husband, she quickly followed her
father, and the three stood side by side. Groans of
disappointment rose from the crowd when the cell
door was closed and they saw that only three were
to be sacrificed instead of six, as they had heard.
The sight of the timid, shrinking form of Melita
seemed to touch the heart of the prefect, however,
with a very different feeling, and, rising from his
seat, he said aloud, speaking to her: "Thou surely
wilt not be so obstinate as to persevere in bringing
this destruction upon thyself."

"Great prefect, my wife will die in the faith of
Christ," said her husband, in reply.

"Sacrifice even now to the gods of Rome, whose
anger ye have kindled by your atheism, and ye

AGGREGATE: *collection*
DEPRAVITY: *wickedness*
PROPENSITIES: *natural inclinations*

shall be set at liberty," said the prefect.

"Nay, that is not possible; for the God whom we serve will not give His glory to another," answered the elder man.

"The Christians to the lions! the Christians to the lions!" shouted the crowd, impatiently.

The prefect lifted his hand and looked at them sternly, while a herald, seeing that look, commanded silence. Marcus Aurelius had given commandment to make every effort to save these foolish, obstinate people, as he thought them; and so, when quiet was once more restored, the prefect said, "This Christ, whom ye profess to serve, cannot save ye from the lion."

"But He has saved us from sin, and will take us speedily to the glory beyond the grave," answered one of the martyrs. "The lion can but destroy these vile bodies; our souls we have already committed to the charge of our God, and how can we take them back? He has redeemed us from the evil of this world and the service of the demons whom ye vainly call gods."

"The Christians to the lions! the Christians to the lions! they insult our gods!" cried a multitude of voices in the crowd.

"It is enough," said the prefect. "I would fain have saved them from the punishment of their folly, but it is all in vain, and they must die to appease the outraged honour of Jupiter."

"They must die, or Rome will be quite ruined," remarked one; "the Tiber overflowing its banks is clearly caused by the atheism of these people."

While he had been speaking the grating had been drawn away from the den of the lion, and the next minute he bounded forth with a terrible roar, his mane bristling, and his eyes ablaze with anger and hunger, for he had been kept without food for the last twenty-four hours. He did not see his victims, however, as he came out; but his eyes falling on that living wall of faces stretching away in the distance, he made a bound at the parapet, as if to reach them, but it was far too high for him to scale, and so, with a deep growl, he ran round it several times, as if in search of some accessible spot. It was not until some movement or sound of those standing in the middle attracted his attention that he saw them. Then he stopped in his run, and, with one deafening roar, sprang upon them.

Melita had fainted in her husband's arms just before that fatal spring, and so she was mercifully spared any further agony, for the lion fell upon her first, tearing her limb from limb before her husband's eyes. He smiled triumphantly when he saw that all pain for her was over.

"My God, I thank Thee that Thou hast heard my prayer!" he cried, with a loud voice. "The sting of death is taken away," he added. "Jesus, receive my spirit!" he cried, as the lion seized him.

A few minutes and all was over. The blood-stained arena, the mangled limbs, and torn shreds of garments showed where the heroic martyrs had been; but they had winged their flight to a land where there is no darkness, and no groping for day; where there can be no mistakes and misrepresentations, for God Himself is King, and shines as the sun in the firmament, and His people rejoice in His light.

CHAPTER III

A NEW CONVERT

SEVERAL months passed away, but there had been few games in the Colosseum since the one in which the Christians had been sacrificed to the popular demand, for dire disasters had visited the Imperial City and its environs, and even the most frivolous had been forced to think of something beyond mere amusement.

The first slight inundation of the Tiber had been followed by another, and now half the lower part of the city lay in ruins. Houses had been thrown down, bridges swept away, vineyards torn up, and cornfields so washed over that the crops had been destroyed; and now another enemy was marching upon the luxurious city. Gaunt and grim famine was near at hand, and the poor, upon whom all these disasters fell most heavily, began to feel the iron hand of this destroyer, and murmurs deep, if not very loud, were uttered against the Christians as the cause of all this ruin. So they had to be more cautious than ever when they ventured

INUNDATION: *flooding*

to assemble for public worship. In the dusk of the evening, however, they ventured to set out in parties of two or three together, and, taking the most circuitous roads, met at last in a large chamber that had been excavated out of the very heart of the Esquiline Hill. The sight of a stranger among them was of rare occurrence now, and caused some little alarm one evening when one appeared. The friends who had brought her, however, hastened to assure their brethren that they had nothing to fear.

"It is an answer to our prayers offered outside the Flavian Amphitheater where our brethren suffered," said one; "for this noble lady, who was present then, was so impressed by the martyrs' firmness that she sought to know more of that religion that could give such courage and raise such hopes. She has learned something of our holy faith from a slave in her service; but she would fain learn more, and she seeks our teaching, my brethren." As the speaker concluded the lady allowed the long dark cloak she wore to fall from her shoulders and removed her veil, disclosing the features of the young matron Flavia. She was not the only patrician lady present, but a start of surprise went through the little company as they noticed her rank; but they bade her welcome in the usual form, and she sat down beside the catechumens or learners, while her slave took her place among the members of the Church.

CIRCUITOUS: *round about*
ESQUILINE HILL: *a residential section of the city of Rome*
CATECHUMENS: *students learning the basics of Christianity*

This underground chamber, with its rough, un-adorned walls and its single smoking lamp, swing-ing from an iron chain in the middle of the roof, was a strange scene to the polished, luxurious lady. There were no statues or altars or censers; nothing that could remind her of the heathen temples or the worship of the popular deities. A venerable-looking old man was seated at a rough wooden desk, on which lay a roll of papyrus, and soon after Flavia entered the whole company rose, and, with upraised eyes and outstretched arms, united silently in the prayer which the old man spoke aloud. Then the roll was opened, and a por-tion of the Gospel of John was read and a hymn sung. After this, instruction was given to the cat-echumens, and among these Flavia took her place, answering the questions that were put to her by her teacher with the same readiness and meek-ness as the rest.

It was a strange class of learners. Beside the pa-trician lady sat a British slave-girl, and next to her a robber, who had once made these same Cata-combs his headquarters, and had been the terror of all the neighbourhood. Then there was a wool-comber; a freedman, who had lived by pandering to the vices of his patron; a hardworking miner, who spent his whole time in fashioning such cham-bers and galleries as this, and to whom the hope of spending an eternity in the sunlight had been the first attraction towards this despised faith. To

CENSERS: *containers for burning incense*
VENERABLE-LOOKING: *dignified*
PANDERING TO THE VICES: *profiting from the sin*

each and all of these the good news of salvation had some special attraction, differing according to their different needs and natures, but working in each the same result—meekness and lowliness, and a desire to enter upon a new life. After the catechumens had been instructed an old man led in some little children, and they, too, were taught that the Lord Christ was waiting to bless them now, as He had blessed the children of Judaea.

When the catechumens were dismissed, Flavia threw the cloak over her shoulders, and following her guide, who carried a lantern to light them through the gloomy passages, slowly left the Church. It had been a blessed season of refreshment to her soul, and she was unwilling to leave, for she knew not when she might be able to come again, as she had already incurred great dangers to be present tonight. This bare, rough-hewn cavern was no common chamber, but the very gate of heaven to her soul, and she felt no horror, no fear, when she saw, on their way back, that this was a burying-place for the dead as well as a meeting-place for the living. All along the passages were little niches cut out of the soft stone, and in each of these lay one or two corpses, many of them those of Christian martyrs, as she could see by the palm branch cut in the stone above and the words "in peace" written underneath. The sight of this brought to Flavia's recollection that scene in the Colosseum, which she could never recall without a shudder, although it had been the turning-point in her own life-history.

Carefully and cautiously they threaded their way up through the labyrinthine passages to a deserted garden, where, concealed among the dark-leaved ilex and olive copse, a trapdoor had been made to afford this secret entrance to the Catacombs. They still had to use caution in passing through this neighbourhood to the more densely inhabited parts of the city, for the place was infested with robbers, and murders were not infrequent here.

At last the more wealthy districts of the city were reached, where Flavia had to be specially careful lest she should be recognized by any of the gay passengers on their way to the palace, on the Palatine Hill, where the Empress Faustina was entertaining a number of guests in honour of the birth of the twin princes who had been born a short time previously. Flavia herself was expected to be present at this festive scene, for they had left the quiet of their villa at Aricia, and taken up their abode in one of the wings of the extensive palace built by Nero, since her husband had entered the service of the emperor. His absence tonight, however, had afforded her the long-desired opportunity of attending the services in the Christian Church, where she hoped to be admitted as a member shortly; but she ran some risk of discovery now on her way home.

LABYRINTHINE: *like a labyrinth or maze*
ILEX: *holly*
COPSE: *wooded area*

The streets were hung with lamps, and several daintily-perfumed and garland-crowned Greeks, on their way to the palace or the house of some friend, paused to look more curiously at the closely enveloped figures of the two women as they glided hastily and cautiously along. There were crowds of miserable beggars, too, many of them holding out deformed or mutilated infants, obtained for the express purpose of exciting the pity of the more fortunate citizens. Alas! it needed no extraneous misery now; the pale, pinched faces told the tale of starvation all too plainly, and Flavia shuddered as she looked from the abject crowd to the gorgeous palace, with its thousand pillars of marble, its triple porticoes, and avenues stretching down each slope of the hill. Such luxury and such misery, thus brought together, the world has rarely seen; and she did not wonder that their emperor, intent on diminishing the one and alleviating the other, should often grow weary and disheartened at the gigantic task he had set himself, or that it needed vigilant sentries and the services of the Prætorian guards to keep all unwelcome intruders out of the palace.

She herself had to be cautious now when she presented herself for admission; but, fortunately, she had no difficulty in this matter, and gained her own private apartments without any mishap. Her sister, Sisidona, who had come to live with her, looked up as she entered the *peristyle.* "What

EXTRANEOUS: *additional*
PERISTYLE: *an open area surrounded by columns*

hath happened, my Flavia?" she asked, in a tone of alarm, hastening to her sister's side as she spoke.

Flavia tried to smile. "Thou art timid tonight, Sisidona," she said.

"Nay, but, my sister, thou art the one frightened, I am sure. Has anything happened to interrupt the banquet?" she asked.

"I have not been to the banquet," said Flavia, colouring as she spoke.

"Not been to the banquet!" uttered the young lady slowly, now noticing, for the first time, that her sister had none of her jewels on, and had made but little change in her dress since the morning.

Flavia looked still more confused as she saw the puzzled expression of her sister's face. "Do not ask me where I have been," she said, hastily. "I will tell thee all by-and-by."

"But what will the empress say?" asked Sisidona, after a lengthened pause.

"She will not miss such a humble guest as myself," answered Flavia, lightly. "Have the children been quite well?" she asked.

"They are well, I think; Flaminia tells me thou hast not let her pray to the Lares and Penates lately; but I insisted upon her doing it tonight," said Sisidona.

"Do not do it again, my sister," said Flavia.

Sisidona started. "Flavia, what dost thou mean? what is all this mystery? something has happened,

LARES AND PENATES: *general household gods*

I am sure, and if thou wilt not tell me what it is, I will ask Flaminius as soon as he returns."

Flavia grew as white as the marble Diana against which she was leaning, at that threat "Sisidona, thou must not do that," she said, in a whisper, her very lips growing pale as she thought of her husband's anger when he should know where she had been.

Sisidona drew herself up proudly. "No Roman matron fears to tell her husband and sister where she has been visiting," she said, sternly.

"I will tell him, and thee, too, Sisidona; but I cannot do so now," said Flavia, with something of her sister's sternness in the tone she used.

"I do not ask to be admitted to thy secrets, but I will not be made thine accomplice by concealing what I know from thy husband," said Sisidona.

"Thou wilt tell Flaminius I have been out tonight instead of going to the banquet?" asked Flavia.

"I will tell him as soon as he returns with the emperor from Lorium," said Sisidona.

Flavia sank down upon a pile of cushions, covered her face with her hands, and moaned in the agony of her spirit. "Oh, my sister, thou knowest not what misery thou wilt bring upon me," she said.

"Nay, but I will save thee from misery if I can," said Sisidona. "Be persuaded, O my Flavia, and tell Flaminius where thou hast been, even if thou wilt not tell me."

But Flavia only shook her head. "I cannot bear it yet," she said; "by-and-by I will—I must do it, but not just now, not just yet. Sisidona, wilt thou keep my secret if I entrust it to thee?" she suddenly asked.

"Nay, I know not that I can give such a promise as thou requirest," she said; then, suddenly bursting into tears, she threw herself upon her sister's shoulder sobbing forth, "Flavia, thou knowest how deeply I love thee, and how Flaminius holds thee as the purest and noblest matron in Rome; surely thou hast not been drawn into the commission of any crimes such as disgrace the palace, pure as our emperor's court is."

Flavia smiled through her tears. "Thou art more foolish than a goose, my little sister," she said; "I am not a fashionable lady, such as a flower-crowned Greek would make love to, neither do I court the notice of anyone but my darling children."

"Then why shouldst thou fear to tell Flaminius where thou hast been?" said Sisidona, again returning to the charge.

Without replying to this Flavia said, "Sit down beside me, Sisidona, and let me tell thee a story;" and taking her sister's hand she held it tightly, and drew her head down upon her shoulder tenderly as she went on: "Thou rememberest the last time I was present at the gladiatorial games?"

"Thou didst not go the last time," interrupted her sister. "Thou hast not been since those obstinate

Christians were given to the lion," she added.

"And I shall never go again," said Flavia, quietly. "Dost thou remember that last scene—the words the brave martyr spoke? He said his God had redeemed him from sin. I knew that this word 'sin' meant impurity and all kinds of evil, and I knew that it was what our Olympian gods delighted in, although it was hateful to everyone who loved truth and virtue. I had begun to hate it before that day—had begun to long for a purity and goodness above and beyond my own; but where could I find it? Not in the world, for our grand old Roman type of virtue is dead, and there are few men like my Flaminius or our emperor. On the summit of Olympus things were worse than in this world, if the histories of our gods be true. Where, then, could I look for purity and goodness but to the God who redeemed His followers from their sins?"

Sisidona started from her sister's sheltering arms as she said this. "Thou dost not mean to say thou hast been seeking the God of the Christians?" she said, in a tone of horror.

Flavia bowed her head. "I have sought and found Him," she said; "and *I* know now that He has redeemed *me* from all sin."

"Flavia, thou art crazed!" said her sister; "tell me, this is all a mistake—some horrible dream, from which we shall awaken presently."

"Nay, nay, it is not a dream, but a blessed reality. I am a Christian, and have been this night to seek

OLYMPIAN GODS: *the Greek gods who, according to Greek mythology, lived on Mount Olympus*

admission to the Christian Church."

She might have said more, but, without one word of reply, Sisidona turned hastily away and went to her own chamber; and Flavia, after a short time, went to look at her children before retiring to rest.

CHAPTER IV

A CONFESSION

WHEN Flavia reached her own room she resolved to seek by prayer the strength she needed to meet the coming trial, for she saw that further concealment was impossible, and it was almost a relief to her mind that she should be thus forced to tell her husband. The bare fact of having a secret she dared not confide to him was in itself a pain and misery to her. This had been enhanced by what she had been compelled to witness and tacitly join in every day, for not a meal could be taken without the gods being acknowledged, and their worship was interwoven with every act of social and domestic life. That she and her slave, Nerissa, had hitherto escaped detection from their remissness in many of these rites and ceremonies was almost a marvel, although they had not been so unnoticed as they imagined.

Before Flavia had concluded her supplications—while she was still standing gazing intently upward—the heavy curtain before the doorway was

TACITLY: *agreeing by not objecting*
REMISSNESS: *neglect*

pushed aside, and Sisidona entered.

"Flavia, I have come to say I will not inform Flaminius of what hath happened tonight," she said, in a cold mechanical voice.

A faint colour stole into Flavia's face. "I will myself inform him as soon as he returns," she said. "I cannot bear this concealment any longer. I have been weak and faithless in hiding this change so long."

"Hast thou thought of Flaminius at all in this matter?" inquired Sisidona, still in the same cold tone.

Flavia bowed her head in her hands, and groaned, "Oh, my sister, what shall I do? I fear to think of the effect of my confession upon my husband."

"It is well thou art not quite heartless—that the gods have not wholly abandoned thee; for, as this matter is a secret known only to me as yet, thy noble husband may still be spared the pain of knowing that his wife, whom he deems the purest matron in Rome, has embraced the faith held only by depraved wretches who make this an excuse for the exercise of cruelty and vice."

"Nay, nay, my sister; this charge is false," interrupted Flavia. "Many, nay most, of the Christians are poor, I know; but they live holy, blameless lives, loving and helping one another in poverty and distress, more than would be thought possible if it were not so strangely true."

"Then thou art determined to take the part of these people?" said her sister.

"How can I do otherwise, when I am one of them, and know that what I say is true?" replied Flavia.

"Flavia, thou must not be so rash as to call thyself a Christian because thou hast been to their place of meeting once."

"Nay, I might go many times, and still remain a worshiper of the old gods; but, my sister, I have learned to love the Christ whom these people love. I believe He is the Saviour who came to redeem me from my sins and the power of evil. It is this that makes me love these people, and long to join with them; for I want to know more of this Saviour's love, and I want to prove that I love Him by forsaking all false gods and serving Him alone."

"Then thou art still determined to forsake the gods of Rome?" said Sisidona, impatiently.

"They are not gods, but demons," Flavia answered, warmly.

"We will not argue this question, my sister; we will leave the gods alone: but, about thy husband—what of him?"

"I will tell Flaminius what I know to be the truth—the truth of God," said Flavia.

"And break his heart with the disgrace thou hast brought upon his name, as well as that of thy children," warmly replied Sisidona. "Oh, my Flavia, if thou hast no pity for thyself in this matter, think of thy children—the disgrace that must be theirs when it is known that their mother is a Christian."

For a few moments Flavia could not speak, and when at last she had sufficiently subdued her emotion to be able to reply, she spoke in a hoarse whisper that told of the agony she suffered: "I have not thought of myself so much as of them—my husband and children, and my Saviour, who has died to redeem them. Think of it, Sisidona. He died to redeem my dear ones—you and Flaminius, and my little Flaminia and Cassius, and yet ye know nothing, care nothing for it; and shall I, now that He has taught me to know it, refuse to love Him in return, and tell you of His love?"

"It will be useless to tell me of anything concerning these Christians," said her sister, "and I can speak for Flaminius also; therefore thou hadst better try and forget all these vain stories that have been imposed upon thee, and spare thy husband the pain and disgrace that must follow the declaring thyself of this vile faith."

Flavia looked at her sister in surprise. Her words were so hard, cold, and unfeeling that she could not believe it was the gentle Sisidona; but nothing daunted, she said, "I must tell Flaminius everything when he returns."

"Then the gods have mercy upon thee, since thou wilt have none upon thyself;" and with a deep-drawn sigh Sisidona left the room.

NOTHING DAUNTED: *not to be discouraged*

Flavia passed an almost sleepless night, for she knew that her sister had not exaggerated the effect her confession was likely to make upon her husband. And yet, agonizing as the thought was that she must bring pain and sorrow to that loving heart, she could not turn back from the path she had entered upon. "It is through much tribulation we must enter the kingdom of light beyond the realm of shades," she whispered softly to herself, "and my trials are light indeed compared with what many have to endure."

Flavia did not know, yet, how deeply she must suffer; how heavy her cross would prove; how long and weary the way would be before the crown was gained; and it was well she could not, for at present the thought of her husband was enough to cause her the deepest anxiety.

When Flaminius returned from Lorium, a few days afterward, he saw that something had happened, and immediately asked if the children were well.

"Yes, they are quite well, and eagerly looking for thy visit to their room," answered Flavia, forgetting her trouble for a few minutes in the joy of his arrival.

"And thou, my Flavia, thou hast not been well, for thou wert not at the banquet given by Faustina."

The lady coloured deeply. "I was not at the banquet because—because I was otherwise engaged," she said, slowly.

SHADES: *the spirits of the dead*

Her husband looked his surprise at her reply. "Thou wert otherwise engaged!" he repeated. "Wilt thou tell me what thou meanest, Flavia?" he added, somewhat sternly.

She sat down on a cushion at his feet, and hid her face on his knees. "I will tell thee everything," she said; "only be patient with me, Flaminius—patient and merciful," she added, pleadingly.

He almost started from his seat at these words. "A Roman matron ask mercy at the hands of her husband!" he said. Then leaning forward he laid his hands tenderly on her head.

"My Flavia, thou art ill, I am sure. The accounts we have heard lately concerning the distress and suffering among the poor by the riverside have been too much for thee. But be comforted, dear heart; the poor have a friend and father, as well as an emperor in Marcus."

"I have thought of the poor lately, Flaminius, but not of them alone; for many of us are poorer than those we deem the poorest. Thou rememberest the Christians who were thrown to the lions? We deemed them miserable, but they were the noblest men in Rome."

Her husband withdrew his hands from her head as she said these last words. "Who has been talking to thee about these miserable atheists?" he asked.

"I know whereof I affirm, for I have learned to know and love the truth which they teach," said Flavia, firmly.

ATHEISTS: *people who do not believe in any god*

She did not look up to see the effect of her words; she only knew that her husband sat quite still without replying to her, and she could not see the look of agony that stole into his face, and how the lips settled themselves as if to guard every word, lest there should be any evidence of the mortal anguish he was called to endure. With arms folded, and scarcely a quickened pulse, he sat and listened, without word or sign, while Flavia told him what she had previously told her sister. At last she ventured to raise her head and look into his face, and with a low cry she flung herself upon his breast as she saw the look of agony depicted there.

"My husband! my Flaminius! I shall love thee more truly—be a better wife to thee, because I am a Christian."

But he put her from him, not roughly or passionately, but firmly and yet with gentleness, as he said, "I have no wife now. *My* Flavia was no Christian; but a noble Roman matron;" and without another word he passed from the room, leaving his wife in a state of grief and perplexity that almost deprived her of her senses.

How long she sat leaning against the marble Diana she did not know, but she crept away to her own room at last; and when her favourite slave, Nerissa, came to prepare her bath, she found her mistress suffering so severely as to be unable to rise from the couch on which she lay. Nerissa knew what had happened, and so, while she bathed her mistress' throbbing temples, she ventured to whisper a few words of comfort and hope.

"The noble Flaminius will relent," she said. "God will change his heart, and he, too, will become a Christian."

Flavia sighed. "I am very weak and faithless, Nerissa," she said. "I am often afraid of myself, that I shall deny my Lord and Saviour."

"It is the weak ones the Lord Christ carries nearest to His heart," said the slave, "and for them miracles are performed if they cannot otherwise be helped."

No one questioned the miracles of Christ in those days; indeed, the early Christians had no doubt but that miracles were still wrought on their behalf; so Nerissa had little fear for her mistress' faithfulness, or that the Gospel, once known, would not be learned by other members of the family. By degrees, Flavia caught something of the girl's hopeful spirit, and after she had rested for an hour she felt so much better as to be able to dress for the evening meal.

To her surprise, her sister only was in the *triclinium*, although the supper was waiting, and, in answer to her inquiries for Flaminius, Sisidona said he was in attendance upon the emperor. How she knew this she did not say, and Flavia did not inquire. Very few words were spoken during the progress of the meal, for the slaves were in

TRICLINIUM: *dining room*

attendance; but when at last the two ladies were left alone, Flavia told her sister that she had informed her husband of the change in her faith.

"And thou couldst break one of the noblest hearts in Rome without feeling and without remorse!" exclaimed Sisidona. "The worst atheism in the world is that of these Christians."

"Flaminius is angry, as I feared he would be; but I shall soon convince him that to be a Christian is to be a better wife and mother, more gentle, more patient, and given less to pleasure," answered Flavia.

Her sister, however, declined to discuss the subject with her, and finding that it was useless to try and draw her into conversation, Flavia went to look at the little sleepers, and breathe a silent prayer to God from her children's pillows on their behalf. It was her nightly custom to do this now, and the slave who had charge of them generally came to meet her mistress with a lamp, for she had to cross a long gallery before reaching the children's apartments; but tonight she seemed to have forgotten her, and Flavia had to find her way alone. To her surprise, when she reached the rooms they, as well as the passage, were in darkness. She moved aside the heavy drapery that hung before the doorway of several chambers, but no light was to be seen, and no one answered to her call. Could the children have been stolen? Such things had often been heard of, and she hastened back to give the alarm

GALLERY: *hallway*

and send for her husband at once. But, to her surprise, the slave to whom she gave this command
only looked at her in blank amazement. "The children are not stolen," he said; "they went away with
their slaves this afternoon."

"Went away from their home, and I was never
consulted!" exclaimed Flavia; and she went in
search of her sister.

Sisidona confirmed the slave's words. Flaminia
and Cassius had been taken away by their father's
orders, but she did not know where they had gone
or when they would return, or when Flaminius
himself might be expected.

Flavia was more alarmed at the loss of her children than she cared to own even to herself. Although she sought to encourage herself in hoping
they would soon return, her anxiety on their account grew more intense as hour after hour passed
and her husband still remained absent.

Sisidona had retired to her own room, and most
of the slaves had gone to bed; but Flavia still waited
in the *peristyle*, sometimes engaged in prayer, and
sometimes pacing up and down between the marble pillars, listening to the splash of the fountain
in the *atrium*, or to the rumble of a distant chariot
as it bore some wealthy citizen homeward after a
late entertainment. But the footsteps she waited
for and so anxiously longed to hear did not come,
and at last, utterly weary with her long watching,
Flavia herself retired to her room, where her faith-

ATRIUM: *the central room in a Roman house, it was open to
the sky and had a pool for collecting rainwater in the
center*

ful slave, Nerissa, was waiting to unrobe her. She, too, had heard of the children's sudden departure from home, and had judged, truly enough, that it was for fear their mother would teach them her new faith that this precaution had been taken. She was not altogether without fear on her own account either now, for several of her fellow-slaves had noticed that she did not sacrifice to the gods, or pour out the usual libations in their honour; and she had overheard some of them talking to-gether about this, and discussing whether or not their master should be informed of it.

What the decision had been she did not know; but if he had any cause to suspect her of holding this Christian faith little mercy would be extend-ed to her; though what she most feared was being separated from her beloved mistress at this time. For her sake she was willing to make any conces-sion that did not involve the worship of the gods; but to sacrifice again to them, and thus rob God of the honour due to Him alone, was impossible.

The fears that had arisen on her own account Nerissa would not impart to her mistress tonight. She had enough to bear in the absence of her children, and the displeasure of her husband and sister; and so Nerissa spoke only words of hope, quoted from the sacred Scriptures, with which she had carefully stored her memory.

LIBATIONS: *offerings of wine*

CHAPTER V

MARCUS AURELIUS

MEANWHILE Flaminius had returned to his duties at the other end of the palace, resolving to keep the fact of his wife's dishonour to himself, at least for the present. He was, however, surprised into taking the emperor into his confidence very soon afterward, for Marcus Aurelius on entering the room was astonished to see his secretary sitting there, and at once divined that something must have happened in his own home for him to return so soon. A slight colour stole into the cheek of the young Roman as the emperor made this inquiry in a tone of deep concern, and he answered, "I am in trouble; the gods have wholly forsaken me."

"Nay, nay; say not so, Flaminius; our gods have but few true worshipers now, I fear. I, who am chief priest as well as emperor, believe in them; but many of the flamens and augurs do not; and as for the people, the ignorant worship because they are ignorant, and most of the philosophers

FLAMENS: *priests*
AUGURS: *fortune-tellers*

sneer at them and at the gods too; so that where there is a true worshiper—a true believer—who, feeling the poverty of his own nature, looks to the gods for help, they are not likely to forsake such."

"But if the one dear to thee as the gods themselves—dearer than life itself—forsakes them openly, and avowedly prefers another and a strange god, what then?" asked Flaminius, fiercely, forgetting that it was the emperor—the high-priest of Jupiter—who stood before him, and remembering him only as the faithful friend.

Marcus Aurelius looked into his troubled, anxious face. "It is thy wife to whom thou art referring. Has she joined the fashionable, frivolous crowd, who prefer the worship of Isis and Serapis to the gods of Rome?" he asked.

"Nay, if it were only that I should not be so troubled," answered Flaminius; "but it is these accursed Christians whom she has chosen to follow."

"The Christians!" repeated the emperor. "Is it possible that any Roman matron could join so depraved and obstinate a sect?"

"They are, indeed, obstinate," said Flaminius; "for the example made of those who were sacrificed to the lion, and which ought to have deterred everyone who witnessed it from meddling with their dangerous doctrines, seems to have been the main cause of my wife joining them."

"Has she joined herself to these people?" inquired the emperor, in an incredulous tone.

AVOWEDLY PREFERS: *openly acknowledges*

"She has been to their place of meeting; she went there instead of attending the banquet given by the empress."

Marcus Aurelius looked perplexed. It was beyond his comprehension to understand how a Roman patrician lady, gentle, modest, and retiring as he knew Flavia was, could wish to consort with slaves, and the lowest and poorest of the people, in preference to being present at a brilliant assemblage of Rome's noblest and most honoured society.

He paced up and down the marble-paved chamber, lost in thought, for several minutes, vainly trying to find some clue to this mystery. "If thy wife had been one of our fashionable ladies I could have understood it better," he said, at length, "for our women vie with each other in splendour and extravagance, even as men plunge headlong into the pursuit of pleasure; and this is the death of all happiness. People grow discontented and wretched with a life that has nothing else to offer them, and eagerly seize upon any mad freak, if only for a change. It was so in the days of Seneca, and things have been growing worse since, so that men rush upon death because they have exhausted every pleasure and every vice."

"But my Flavia was not one of these," said Flaminius, when the emperor paused. "She loved the society of her children better than the gayest assemblage or the most splendid entertainment."

SENECA: *a Roman philosopher in the first century* A.D.

"If ever she can be won to give up this detestable faith it will be through her affection for her children," said the emperor.

"I have told her she shall be my wife no longer," said Flaminius, mournfully.

"That is well. Be firm in this, and remove the children with their slaves for a time, lest she should try to imbue their young minds with a love of this strange god."

Marcus Aurelius did not mean to be unkind. He was one of the most gentle and amiable men, and he firmly believed that he was doing not only the wisest but the kindest thing possible for Flavia, as well as for her husband. For this young secretary he felt a most sincere regard; and, anxious that no time should be lost, he dispatched Flaminius at once to make arrangements for his children's removal from their mother, and at the same time ordered him to take up his abode at the end of the palace.

When Flaminius returned, an hour later, the children were already on their way to Aricia, and he was ready to commence any business the emperor might have in hand. There was little fear but that he would find abundant occupation, for the emperor himself was literally a hardworking man, and found employment for several secretaries to write letters on the various subjects of which he took the active oversight himself. The state of the roads in various parts of the kingdom—the

IMBUE: *fill*

choice of just and faithful men as prefects and magistrates—the equal distribution of the imperial allowance of corn—even the regulation of street traffic in the Imperial City, all came under his notice, besides the weightier matters concerning the government of so many and such various distinct provinces.

Today a messenger had arrived from Britain bringing tidings of another revolt. "These islanders are difficult to conquer," remarked Flaminius.

"They have never been entirely subdued, not because they were more brave or better warriors than the Gauls, but because Rome has grown feeble, and her policy toward this half-subdued people has varied with each of her emperors," said Marcus Aurelius. "I shall follow that of my noble predecessor. They must be taught to worship the gods of Rome; as well as to receive our arts and laws. There is already a temple dedicated to Diana in our colony of Londinium, and one to Apollo just beyond the walls; but the islanders themselves hold fast to their own savage worship."

"Each nation must have its own gods," remarked Flaminius, "and it were well if each kept to its own; but since the Jews first came to Rome, there has been trouble through their religion;" and he sighed as he spoke.

"The Jews hate these Christians as deeply as thou dost," said the emperor; and thinking it would be better to turn the thoughts of the secretary toward the business now claiming attention, he directed how several letters should be written so that they might be ready for him to seal with his own hand early in the morning.

With the parchment spread before him, and the reed balanced on his finger, Flaminius gave himself a few moments to think of the terrible cloud that had suddenly gathered over all his hopes of happiness. "This will darken all my days," he said half-aloud; then remembering that the messenger was to depart for Britain early the following morning, he commenced writing his letters, for some, at least, must be finished before he went to take his daily bath.

Flaminius was a busy man, and could not find time to bathe more than once a day; but many of the fashionable and gay young men of Rome bathed three or four times, spending the whole day from dawn to dark at the baths; for here there were not only rooms for ablution, and slaves to assist in the dressing afterward, but libraries, gardens, tennis courts, and usually a theater, all under one roof. These public baths had originally been intended for the use of the poorer citizens, as the wealthy had them in their own houses. But they had gradually come to be most popular places of resort to meet with friends, pass an idle hour, or lounge away the whole day, as suited best, for the baths were convenient for either.

ABLUTION: *washing*
RESORT: *relaxation*

As Flaminius was writing he suddenly remembered that he had promised to meet a friend in the vestibule of the baths just beyond the Forum, the most fashionable and splendid in Rome, and patronized by many living in the palace in preference to those within the palace walls. There was little fear that Marcinius had left, for he was one of those gossips who spent most of their time in bathing and talking the fashionable scandal of the day.

Marcinius had hinted that he had something of importance to tell him, and Flaminius, with a smile at the thought of anything being important that Marcinius knew, had promised to meet him as he desired, and now, for his word's sake, he felt compelled to go, although he would greatly have preferred not to meet anyone just at present. Even after he had left the palace he was inclined to turn back, and at the golden milestone, near the Forum, where all the roads of Italy met, he turned half-round to retrace his steps. But, ashamed of his indecision, the next minute he hurried on, not pausing again until the marble portico of the building was reached.

Here several acquaintances met Flaminius, but he fancied their greetings were cold, and that they looked at him curiously. As he paused for a moment at the entrance to pay his money and receive an admission ticket he felt sure that several of the loungers looked round after him, and was somewhat annoyed, although he resolved not to let

VESTIBULE: *entrance hall*

anyone suspect his annoyance. Marcinius, he saw, was not in the vestibule, and so Flaminius strolled to a spacious chamber beyond, where those about to take a bath were preparing themselves for their luxurious ablutions.

It was a splendid room; the mosaic pavement was of the costliest marbles, while its walls were divided into panels or compartments, each painted in fresco to match the floor, while long casements, reaching from the ceiling, admitted a chastened light into every part of the room.

As Flaminius entered there was a little burst of applause from the crowd of loungers at the upper end of the room, and on going nearer he found that one of the numerous poets of the day was reading his latest production to an admiring audience. Flaminius, however, who had little taste for such things, did not stay longer than to satisfy himself that Marcinius was not of the number, and then turned to look round among the waiting slaves for his friend.

He was not to be seen, however, and so Flaminius began to prepare for his own bath by taking off his clothes, which were hung on a peg near the entrance, and receiving from one of the attendant slaves a long loose robe. He passed to a second smaller chamber, which was heated to a voluptuous warmth. This, too, was nearly full; some of those reclining in almost speechless lassitude, be-

MOSAIC: *pictures formed by small pieces of stone and glass*
FRESCO: *plaster painted while it is still wet*
CASEMENTS: *windows*
CHASTENED: *subdued*

ing about to take their third or fourth bath that day; many of them so enervated as to be unable or unwilling to rise and greet a friend who might come in. Here Flaminius would have to wait some little time, and he hoped to see Marcinius enter, for the bathers reclined in this chamber both before and after the bath.

But Flaminius was too impatient to wait long today, even in this luxurious room; and as he rarely indulged in the preparatory vapour bath he proceeded to plunge into the marble basin of tepid or rather warm water, over which delicate perfumes were profusely scattered. Marcinius, meanwhile, who always brought his own slaves with him, was but in the adjoining chamber enjoying the additional luxury of the vapour bath. This was always accompanied by an exhalation of choice perfumes, and after it the bather was seized by his slaves, who scraped and rubbed him until he was partially cooled, and then passed again to the heated chamber, where the real luxury of the process was commenced.

The slaves anointed the bathers, from vials of gold or alabaster, with the choicest perfumes and unguents that the art of man could compound; and while he was still undergoing this Flaminius saw Marcinius enter, and he beckoned to him at once.

The young man, who could boast of being more

VOLUPTUOUS: *physically pleasing*
LASSITUDE: *lazy indifference*
ENERVATED: *weak*
UNGUENTS: *ointments*

lavish of gold and more deficient in brains than any of his companions, languidly seated himself near Flaminius, and said with a yawn, "I thought thou wert never coming."

"I have been busy," said Flaminius, curtly.

Marcinius shrugged his shoulders. "It is a weariness for me to get to the baths; I would not be troubled with any man's business—"

"Or trade," interrupted Flaminius, with a spice of mischief in his tone, for he knew that, in spite of the airs Marcinius gave himself, his father's ears had been bored, and he had sat in the slave market, and that he gained his enormous wealth by a trade which every patrician despised and held to be ignoble.

"No, I would not be troubled with trade or business either," said Marcinius. "Life at the best is but a weariness;" and he sighed as though he found the burden almost insupportable.

"Thou hadst a matter of some importance to consult me upon," said Flaminius, after a lengthened pause.

"Yes, but I suppose thou hast heard it long since, for everybody was talking of it."

"Talking of what?" asked Flaminius.

"Of thy wife," answered Marcinius.

Flaminius started to his feet, throwing down two of the slaves who were anointing him. "Who dared to mention the name of my wife?" he demanded.

LANGUIDLY: *lazily*
HAD BEEN BORED: *pierced as a sign of slavery*
IMPIETY: *disrespectfulness to God or a god*

"Everybody is doing it—she is the talk of Rome; for it is no secret that she favours these Christians who have brought all these calamities upon us by their impiety. Indeed, I have heard that she is a Christian herself," added Marcinius, spitefully, glad of an opportunity of retaliating for some of the slights and insults he was continually receiving from Flaminius and other patricians.

It was like receiving a mortal wound for Flaminius to hear that his pure and noble wife had become the common talk of these gossips. To many it would have been no degradation—they would have seen no dishonour in it; but Flaminius was not one of these. He made little pretensions to wealth or distinction beyond what his patrician rank gave him; but his grand, true, old Roman sense of honour was very fine, very sensitive, and for men to breathe the name of his Flavia in their common everyday talk was to tarnish her fair fame, to sully the purity of his spotless wife.

For a moment he felt ready to strike this driveling son of a slave dead at his feet, but he curbed his passionate emotion, and bidding the slaves to hasten over the remainder of their task he turned away from Marcinius without uttering a word, greatly to the other's disappointment, who longed to tell him that he himself had tracked her footsteps to the deserted garden, where he had overheard a few whispered words that informed him of her errand there, and that there

DEGRADATION: *extreme disgrace*
SULLY: *stain*
DRIVELING: *drooling, talking stupidly*

was a secret entrance to the Catacombs close at hand.

All this he had intended to tell Flaminius and watch how he received this tale of dishonour; but the patrician had turned proudly away without asking a single question, and so the information was given unasked to a neighbour on the other side, but loud enough for Flaminius to hear some portion of it before he escaped to the outer room beyond the reach of his tormentor's voice.

CHAPTER VI

PERSECUTION

SLOWLY and thoughtfully Flaminius retraced his steps toward the palace, gloomily pondering over the bitter disgrace his wife had brought upon him. That men like Marcinius should have the power of stinging him as he had that day been stung was well nigh unendurable to the proud patrician, and he almost wished he could leave Rome, that no one might again be able to point to him and say his wife was a Christian.

Still pondering thus he reached the Palatine Hill and as he passed the entrance leading to his own dwelling he paused for a minute to consider whether he should go in and see Flavia, to reproach her for what she had done, and try to persuade her to refute the accusation that had been brought against her by publicly sacrificing in the temple of Jupiter the next day. He feared, however, that the attempt would be useless when he considered how obstinate these Christians always proved, and he resolved to give up the attempt for the present, hoping that the absence of himself and the children would prove sufficient to induce her to give up this new faith very shortly.

He remembered, before retiring to rest, that he would have to attend the emperor in the Forum early the next morning, and that he had heard that there would be several difficult cases brought up for judgment. He therefore finished writing his letters, and placed his waxen tablets and stylus all ready for use the next day, for he knew that Marcus Aurelius was no sluggard, and would be at the Forum early.

It was a grand and imposing procession that passed up the Capitoline Hill to the temple, for Marcus Aurelius would not sit in judgment upon any man until he had sacrificed to the gods; and so, in the white vestments of his office as high-priest, attended by his twelve lictors, and followed by the equites, magistrates, and assessors, in their robes, he went to the Temple of Jupiter. Here, in the center of the temple, with Juno on his right and Minerva on his left side, the Thunderer was seated on a throne of gold, grasping the lightning with one hand, and in the other wielding the scepter of the universe. The whole temple was ablaze with gold and jewels; the plunder of the world was lavished here; and the ignorant multitudes might well stand in awe when they ventured to approach their guardian deity. Around the temple stood cattle wreathed with garlands of flowers, while

LICTORS: *officials who carried bundles of rods with an axe in the center, symbolizing the magistrates' power*
EQUITES: *members of the middle class in Rome*

on the steps and in the porticoes were groups of white-robed priests, flamens, and augurs, employed in various parts of the temple service, and looking with supreme disdain and contempt upon those who came to bring their offerings and seek help in their distress from this mighty ruler of the world. All, however, stood aside as the high-priest slowly ascended the long flight of steps, and men bowed their heads as much before the man as the *priest* and *emperor*, for all recognized in Marcus Aurelius a purity and virtue such as the world has rarely seen. When the temple service was over he hastened to lay aside his robes as *pontifex maximus*, and now, arrayed in the imperial purple, bordered with gold, he proceeded to the Forum to hear such cases as came within the province of the chief justice.

Seated in the judgment hall, a prisoner was brought before him who had appealed to be heard by him in a case on the merits of which the other judges could not agree. By an ancient law it was decreed that if a prisoner was met by the Vestal Virgins while on his way to prison he was to be set at liberty. This a prisoner had claimed, but his claim was refused. He had been arrested for debt, and was thrown into prison, notwithstanding that a sacred procession of the six virgins from the temple of Vesta passed him on his way thither; and he now appealed to Cæsar, as judge, to decide the case. Before judgment could be given, however,

ASSESSORS: *assistants to the magistrates*
VESTAL VIRGINS: *highly honored priestesses at the temple of the goddess, Vesta, in Rome*

the other side must be heard, and the creditor had employed an orator to do this, so that it seemed very unlikely that a poor man who could only state the facts for himself would be successful. The orator began by stating that the prisoner was a vine-dresser of Aricia, and had been able to support his family in comfort before he got acquainted with some miserable tufa diggers, who had taught him the atheism that brought ruin on himself and hundreds of others. He boldly declared that he was a Christian now, the orator said, and having called the gods of Rome demons, he had no right to claim mercy in the name of any of their priest-esses.

This was the sum total of the defense, and the orator looked round for the support of the bystand-ers as he finished speaking. The emperor himself looked perplexed, but the people were troubled with no doubts upon the matter, and there was an ominous mutter of, "The Christian to the lions, or Rome will be ruined!" This cry, however, was instantly stopped, and Marcus Aurelius asked the man what he had to say to the charge.

"I am a Christian, it is true," he replied; "but I am a Roman likewise, and claim the protection of her laws."

"Nay, but being an atheist—a believer in a for-eign god whom Rome will never acknowledge—thou dost forfeit all the privileges of a Roman free-man," interrupted the orator.

TUFA: *a soft rock cut into blocks and used extensively by the ancient Romans in construction*

"But I am expected to obey her laws; nay, I have no wish to disobey them," said the man; "for my Divine Master Himself hath taught us to 'Render therefore unto Cæsar the things which are Cæsar's, and unto God the things that are God's.'[1] I, therefore have appealed unto Cæsar. I am willing to pay all my debt if they are patient with me; but since my vines have been destroyed I have not been able to do more than earn a morsel of bread for my wife and children by tufa digging, and how, then, shall I pay this debt?"

"The man speaks reasonably enough," said Marcus Aurelius; "thou dost admit that the sacred virgins met him, and by that meeting he was free; wherefore, then, have ye detained him?"

"Because he was a Christian," the orator ventured to reply.

Marcus Aurelius frowned. "I would that they served the gods of Rome, but they do not, to their loss; but it shall not be that by this they lose their rights as Roman citizens. I demand that they obey the laws of Rome, and I claim for them the protection of the law. The man is free." Having said which the emperor resumed his seat amid the silence of the people, while the prisoner, with a lightened heart, hastened to join his friends outside.

Flaminius sat near the emperor taking notes of the case, and was greatly disturbed when he heard that the man was a Christian. He had known him some years—known him to be an earnest believer

[1] MATTHEW 22:21

in the gods, and yet he had embraced this infamous faith. What was the charm in it? Was it simply infatuation that made people willing to endure disgrace and endless small persecutions from friends and neighbours for the sake of it? or was there really another God greater than Jupiter, as these people pretended? This thought was scouted almost as soon as it arose, and Flaminius almost despised himself for having even momentarily questioned the power of the great deity.

There was, however, another and a nearer cause for being disturbed by the fact that this vinedresser had become a Christian, for his wife was the sister of Flavia's maid, Nerissa, and she often visited their villa while they lived at Aricia, and might have breathed something of this detestable doctrine then. Could it be possible that his wife had thus been contaminated? He resolved to question the vinedresser himself about this, and for that purpose resolved to discover where he lived. Perhaps, too, he might discover what the secret rites of these Christians were; for it might be that one of his children had been sacrificed to this God whom they worshiped, and who demanded human sacrifices on His altar.

Full of this thought, Flaminius quitted the Forum as soon as the business of the day was over, and leaving the region of the palace behind, he plunged into the booth-lined streets, and made his way to the poorest quarter of the town, where many of the tufa diggers lived. Flaminius shivered

INFAMOUS: *detestable*
INFATUATION: *a short-lived but passionate attraction*

at the desolation that reigned in this quarter of the town. The river had rushed from its proper bed, and sweeping down every tenement, had left it a heap of ruins, plowing the ground into holes, and half-burying the wrecks of the miserable dwellings in sand and mud. It had retired now, and the poor creatures who had thus been driven from their homes were venturing back again to see what could be saved from the general ruin. Men were digging out beams of wood to construct other dwellings, while the women pulled out articles of furniture, bronze and earthen pots, though most of the latter were broken and useless.

Flaminius asked one of the men if he knew a vinedresser who had lately come from Aricia to live in that neighbourhood. For a moment the man looked at him questioningly, and then a dark frown gathered on his brow.

"You, too, are one of those who have provoked the anger of our gods and brought this misery upon us," he said, fiercely.

"Nay, by the helmet of Cæsar, I love not these Christians," answered Flaminius.

"But this vinedresser whom ye seek is a Christian," said the man.

"You know him, then," said Flaminius, impatiently; "is he, too, labouring here?" and he looked round upon the other groups as he spoke.

"Nay, nay; but we have driven those Christians from among us, and they have begun to clear a

SCOUTED: *rejected scornfully as absurd*
TENEMENT: *run-down house*

space lower down;" and as he spoke he pointed in the direction where the river had made a wider sweep, and seemed to have done even more damage than where they were standing.

Flaminius did not wait to ask for further directions, but walked on between the holes and hillocks and scattered wrecks of houses toward the spot indicated. Miserable indeed was the aspect of everything here. The river, in retreating, had left the place full of little pools and lakes, while it had swept almost everything portable away in its resistless flow, and if the little colony of Christians wanted to build their houses, or rather hovels, again, they would have to go elsewhere for materials, for there were none to be had there.

Flaminius noticed this, and at the same time remarked that, in spite of all these difficulties, the men who were there seemed to be working heartily and even cheerfully. A temporary shed had already been put up for the accommodation of the women and children, and these, with the old and infirm, seemed to be tenderly cared for. Stepping up to one of the old men, who was hobbling about on a stick, and doing what he could to help carry a log to its place, he asked if he knew Plautius, the vinedresser.

"Yes, indeed I do," answered the man, "for he has been a good friend to me, although so poor and unfortunate himself, for—"

But Flaminius was in no mood to listen to the praises of one who was said to be a Christian, and

ASPECT: *appearance*

hastily interrupted him, saying:

"Lead me to him, old man," at the same time holding out a handful of sesterces as payment. But the old man shook his head at the proffered reward.

"No, no," he said, "I am poor, it is true, but I have left off begging and learned to labour with my own hands since I have begun to love the Lord Christ."

"Lead me to Plautius, and hold thy peace," said Flaminius, impatiently.

"I can lead thee to his wife, but Plautius himself is at work today," said the old man.

"Nay, but he was brought before the emperor this morning," said Flaminius.

"And he went to his work of tufa digging at noon. He has a wife and children to feed, and there are houses to be built by those who understand the work, so that all who can must go to the Catacombs to supply the place of those who are building."

While he had been speaking his guide had led the way to a large lean-to, or shed, where there was a party of women and children, some nursing their infants, some mending a pile of tattered garments that lay beside them, while one or two were making coarse barley cakes and baking them in the ashes of a large fire near the entrance. But although they were thus variously engaged, they were all singing in concert with the children, who were gathered in a group around an old man

SESTERCES: *Roman coins made of brass*
PROFFERED: *offered*

whom they seemed to regard with reverence and affection.

The wife of Plautius saw Flaminius approaching, and rose to meet him, fearing something must have happened to her sister. She looked slightly confused as he paused at the entrance, and a vision of their comfortable cottage in the valley rose before her.

"Things have changed with us, most noble Flaminius," she said, by way of apology, finding that he did not speak.

"Changed indeed! All things are changing, I wot, since the gods of Rome are to be hurled from their seats to make room for this Jewish impostor, who was crucified like a vile slave under Pontius Pilate," said Flaminius, with angry emphasis.

"They are not gods, but demons, and the Lord Christ must reign supreme," said the woman, half-timidly.

Flaminius smiled in derision. The idea was too absurd, too preposterous, for him to contradict; and he said:

"I came not to talk of this foolishness which thou callest Christianity, but to ask some questions; but Plautius, I hear, has gone to work in the Catacombs."

"Yes, now that he is at liberty again he is glad to help, for we have been kept by the brethren while he was in prison," replied the woman. "But if I can answer the questions I will do so."

Flaminius looked at her doubtfully. "Thou wilt

WOT: *know*
DERISION: *contempt*

swear by the gods to tell me truly what I ask?" he said.

"Nay, I cannot swear; but a Christian ever speaks the truth," answered the woman.

"Then thou wilt tell me truly whether Nerissa, my slave, has learned aught of these new doctrines from thee or thy husband?" said Flaminius.

She smiled a little at the question.

"My sister came to our cottage to teach, not to learn," she answered. "Nerissa is a slave in thy household, most noble Flaminius, but she has long been a free-born citizen of the kingdom of light, and sought to bring us to a knowledge of the same truths; but all her efforts were in vain until we saw the courage of the martyrs who were sacrificed to the lion, and from that day both my husband and myself have believed this to be the truth of God."

How much more the woman might have said Flaminius did not wait to hear, but turning away with an impatient gesture of disgust he hurried back to the Palatine Hill.

"They are certainly a strange people—the strangest people in the world," he muttered; "the very thing that would deter most people from embracing their faith seems to prove an attraction to them. Nerissa, too, is a Christian—the most faithful and trustworthy slave of my household has embraced this detestable faith, and my wife has joined in its awful mysteries. I may well complain that the gods have forsaken me," he added, with a deep-drawn sigh.

CHAPTER VII

THROUGH EVIL REPORT

SLOWLY the hours dragged along to Flavia, who waited for tidings of her husband and children, and yet dared not ask for either in the presence of her slaves—dared not to show that she was anxious about them, except to the trusted Nerissa, for fear they should suspect what had taken place. Sisidona was busy about her own concerns, for she was soon to become the wife of Claudius Rufus, who had accompanied them to the Colosseum, and to whom Flavia had given a word of mock-warning concerning her sister becoming a Christian. The young lady was now somewhat perplexed as to whether she ought to inform Claudius of what had taken place; and while two or three slaves were busying themselves about her hair as she sat in front of the bright steel mirror and watched their performance, she was debating with herself whether she could confess that her sister had brought disgrace upon the whole family.

TIREWOMAN: *lady's maid*

"I ought to tell him, I suppose," she thought.

"Hand me that box of gold dust," said her principal tirewoman.

"Don't spare the gold," said Sisidona; "for Claudius loves to see my hair shine and glisten."

"Nothing can be more becoming to my beautiful mistress than this last fashion of doing the hair in the form of a helmet!" exclaimed the woman, in pretended rapture as she proceeded to shake the shining dust adroitly in among the coils of fair hair.

Sisidona surveyed the cumbrous pile of false and real hair with a smile of satisfaction. "Yes, I like it very well. Has Flaminius returned yet?" she asked; for if her brother-in-law did not bring her lover home with him today all this trouble would be wasted.

"Nay, my noble master has gone with the emperor to the Forum," answered the woman, putting in another silver bodkin to secure the pile from toppling over.

By the time Sisidona's dress was all arranged the emperor would have returned to the palace, she knew, and therefore Flaminius might be expected shortly, and so the young lady went to the *peristyle* to await his coming, amusing herself meanwhile with a couple of tame serpents. These were the favourite pets of Flaminius and his wife, and Sisidona knew that her brother-in-law would stay to caress them as soon as he entered, and during this

ADROITLY: *skillfully*
CUMBROUS: *bulky, jumbled*
BODKIN: *hairpin*

time she hoped to learn what he proposed doing in the present state of affairs, and to ask his advice about informing Claudius of Flavia's disgrace.

But to her surprise an hour passed, and still Flaminius did not come, She grew tired of playing with the serpents, and the slave who had charge of them carried them back to their cage, and Sisidona went to her sister's chamber to inquire about Flaminius.

But Flavia could tell her nothing. She, too, had dressed in anticipation of his arrival, but he had not come; and she had noticed that there was a great deal of mysterious whispering among the slaves this morning, and she mentioned this to her sister.

"Then they suspect thee," said Sisidona; "and if thou dost not soon prove to them that thou art a faithful worshiper of Jupiter by sacrificing to him, all Rome will hear of thy disgrace and degradation."

"All Rome may hear that I am a Christian, but it is no disgrace—no degradation," said Flavia, calmly.

Sisidona looked at her pale, placid face, and wondered what could give her strength to endure, for that she was suffering deeply she could see, although she made no remark about the absence of her husband and children. For a moment Sisidona's heart was touched with pity for her sister, but the next minute she had steeled it with the thought that it was only her own obstinacy that caused

PLACID: *calm, peaceful*

this, and that it might also bring disgrace and sorrow not only on her husband and children, but on all connected with her. She was just turning away without having uttered a word of comfort or sympathy when the heavy curtain before the entrance was hastily pushed aside, and Nerissa rushed in panting and frightened. "Save me! save me!" she gasped, throwing herself at her mistress' feet.

"What is it? what has happened?" asked Flavia, in a voice scarcely less agitated.

"Speak quickly, Nerissa," commanded Sisidona. "Dost thou not see that thou art making thy mistress ill?"

"My master, my master!" gasped the girl, and she burst into tears.

Flavia, knowing how much cause she had to fear

discovery and disgrace, looked down upon her pityingly, but her sister grew impatient.

"I will go myself to the *atrium* and discover what has happened, Flavia," she said; "and if it is only some foolish quarrel with the other slaves I would have her punished, if I were her mistress."

When the two were left alone Nerissa raised her streaming eyes to the lady's face and ventured to kiss her hand. "My master has discovered that I am a Christian," she said, "and has sold me."

The lady started, and almost fell to the ground. "Sold thee!" she repeated.

"Yes, I am sold to a Thessalian slave-merchant," answered Nerissa, trying to conquer her emotion.

Flavia could not speak. She was powerless to help the poor girl who had served her so faithfully, and whom she had learned to love as her sister in Christ, in spite of their difference in rank, and she covered her face with her hands and groaned aloud. "My poor girl! my poor Nerissa!" she managed to say at last, "I can but pray for thee, as thou wilt pray for me. Surely the Lord Christ will not tarry long. He will speedily come in glory and convince the world that He is the King of all the earth, and that idols must perish before Him," she added, quickly.

Nerissa shook her head. "I know not, I cannot tell," she said. "The brethren have hoped and believed the Lord was at hand for many weary years, and still He does not come." There was a touch of impatience in the tone, and her mistress detected it.

"The Lord Christ is more patient than we are," she said. "The brethren would have no delay; but what would become of me and many others who are learning thus late to believe in and love Him? Nerissa, it may be in mercy He thus tarries. It may be that the world is to learn slowly, instead of all at once, that the Lord Christ is the Saviour of men."

"Nay, but look at the temple of Jupiter and our bare chamber in the Catacombs. Nothing less than the overpowering glory of our King can throw down the one and exalt the other to its place."

"But think, Nerissa, of the hundreds and thousands who worship Jupiter," said the lady, with a shiver of fear as she reflected that her husband, and the emperor, and many of Rome's bravest and noblest sons, would cleave the closer to this fallen idol, because they would not forsake a failing cause. "It may be in mercy the Lord delays His coming," she added. "It may be that He would rather convert men by His grace than convince them merely by His power and glory."

"But it is the hope of all the Church everywhere—this speedy coming of our Lord," persisted Nerissa. "We constantly pray for it, too," she added, "and therefore we ought to expect it, for He will surely fulfill His promise."

"Yes, He will fulfill His promise, and we ought to pray for and expect His appearing, but we should pray in patience and wait in patience," said Flavia, gently.

Nerissa looked up. She had been the teacher

CLEAVE: *cling*

and her mistress the scholar hitherto, but they seemed all at once to have changed places. The lady noticed the look and tried to smile.

"The Lord Christ will be my Teacher now, Nerissa," she said. "I think He began His teaching last night, when I was sorrowing so sorely for my husband and children. I shall need Him to be my Teacher now," she went on, with a quiver in her voice, "for, kind and faithful as thou art, my Nerissa, thou knowest not the pain of being separated from those so near and dear; and I greatly fear my Flaminius will keep his word now, unless the Lord should change his heart, as He has changed mine."

"My noble mistress, forgive me for my selfishness in coming to thee with my trouble, when thou hast so much more to bear," said Nerissa.

"We each have our own burdens to bear, our own cross to carry; but although I might sink beneath thine, and thou under mine, the Lord Christ can help us each," said the lady, tenderly. "Farewell, Nerissa," she added, as the curtain was again drawn aside. "The Lord Christ watch between us until we meet again, and bless thee for all thou hast taught me!"

The slave who had entered with a message from her master forgot her errand, and stood as if transfixed as she heard these words, and saw the loving caress her mistress bestowed upon Nerissa.

The poor girl guessed the import of her errand. "I am coming," she said, choking back her sobs

IMPORT: *meaning*

and slowly rising to her feet.

"My master is in haste to depart," said the slave, and left the apartment, while Nerissa once more bade her mistress a sorrowful farewell.

Lonely indeed the lady would be when her faithful slave had gone, for it was all too evident from the message sent that her husband had no intention of coming himself to her chamber, and she hardly knew whether to seek him yet, or to await patiently until his anger had somewhat cooled toward her. She resolved, therefore, to wait awhile, and then if he left his home again she would question Sisidona as to what had passed, for she would doubtless have heard all about it. She would inquire, too, which of the slaves had betrayed Nerissa's secret, for that it was one of their own household she had not the least doubt.

With this intention she entered her sister's room an hour or two later, and at her request Sisidona dismissed the slave in attendance for a few minutes, telling her to come in again when she should clap her hands, as she wished to make some alteration in her dress before going to the other end of the palace.

"Art thou going to Flaminius?" asked Flavia, a faint colour stealing into her cheeks as she spoke.

"Yes," answered Sisidona. "There is an entertainment in the circus given by the empress;" and she went to her casket of jewels and took out those she intended to wear.

"Did Flaminius have any message for me, or say

CIRCUS: *a circular arena*
CASKET: *small box*

anything about the children?" Flavia ventured to ask.

"He said the children would not return yet—not until thou hadst given up all thou hadst learned from thy slave Nerissa."

"Who betrayed Nerissa's secret—which of our slaves?" asked the lady, eagerly.

Sisidona's face flushed at the question. "I wish our household slaves had told their master this secret," she said, "instead of letting it become the talk of Rome."

"My sister, what meanest thou?" asked Flavia, in surprise.

"Art thou so much astonished to hear this?" exclaimed the young lady. "I can tell thee more than this, Flavia; thou thyself art the common talk at the baths and in the streets. Everybody has heard of our disgrace, and—"

"Peace, Sisidona!" interrupted her sister. "I am a Christian, it is true; but it is no disgrace to become a servant of the King of kings."

A merry mocking laugh greeted this reply. "Thy King of kings will never reign in Rome," said the young lady. "Thy Church of the Catacombs will never dare to show its head above ground."

"Nay, but when the names of Jupiter and Apollo are forgotten, that of Christ will be a power greater than any the world has yet seen," answered Flavia; "for He will reign from the rising to the setting sun, and all the world will trust in Him as their Saviour God."

"Thou art certainly very strange," said her sister, gazing at the earnest face, and forgetting either to pity or deride her for a minute or two.

Flavia saw her opportunity. "Oh, my sister, if thou couldst but know the blessedness of those who have taken Christ as their Saviour, believing He is their sin and sorrow bearer, thou wouldst seek to know Him for thyself, and—"

"Nay, nay, Flavia, I must not listen to this," interrupted her sister; "and thou must try to forget all thou hast learned concerning this Jewish impostor, now that Nerissa has gone."

"Poor Nerissa! where have they taken her?" asked Flavia.

"Flaminius has sold her, as she doubtless told thee; for it was useless to try and beat this atheism out of her," replied Sisidona; and clapping her hands, she summoned her waiting-maid to assist her in dressing, hoping her sister would not try to introduce the subject of her religion into their conversation again.

Flaminius hoped that by selling Nerissa, and depriving his wife of the society of her children for some time, she would forget the strange doctrines she had learned. He hoped, too, that the scandal concerning her visit to the Catacombs would die out and be forgotten. That he might not hear it mentioned again he took care not to go to the baths, where all the gossip of the day was talked over. In both these expectations, however, he was disappointed. Flavia's non-appearance at the temples was remarked and commented upon, and although this might have been forgotten if she had attended the usual entertainments with her husband, her long-continued absence, coupled with the fact that Flaminius did not reside in the same quarter of the palace as his wife, made the whole affair such a mystery that people were always making inquiries of him or Sisidona concerning the absent lady. These inquiries it was difficult enough to answer for some time; but at length they could say truly enough that Flavia was ill, for the brave spirit had succumbed at last, or rather the weak flesh had given way under the long-continued neglect and unkindness of her husband, and she had, as she thought, lain down on her couch to die.

Flaminius was greatly alarmed when he heard of the dangerous condition of his wife. He had never seen her since the day she had confessed to being a Christian, and he was startled at the change these weeks of anxiety and sorrow had wrought in her when he ventured into her chamber one day, while she was asleep.

"Sisidona!" he said, in an agonized whisper; "we must save her at any cost. I will order a costly sacrifice to be made at the Temple of Fortune, and will inquire of the physician the special cause of this illness; and whatever it may be, it shall be removed!" He winced as he said this, for Sisidona had been the bearer of more than one message from his wife praying that their children might be restored to her. But the same message had always been returned: she must give up this newfound God if she wished to see her children, and if she loved Him more than them, they would be better at a distance from her. Flaminius hoped and expected she would give up what he considered a mere obstinate idea, and when he found it was not, he tried to persuade himself that Flavia was heartless, and had little love for either himself or their children.

To see her, therefore, prostrate through the sufferings so silently and patiently borne that no one knew she had suffered at all, was a shock to him, and he grew hourly more anxious as she continued to grow worse rather than better. Her physician in attendance prescribed herbs and charms, but without effect; and at last Sisidona ventured to suggest that the children should be sent for, a suggestion that was instantly complied with. This proved more efficacious than anything else, and Flavia gradually began to regain strength. At one time it was thought that her illness had effected what her husband so ardently desired, but they were soon undeceived, for she positively refused to pour out a libation to the gods. But Flaminius had resolved to leave her alone in the matter of religion, and, if she still persevered in her determination to be a Christian, to seek from the emperor an appointment in one of the provinces, and leave Rome forever.

PROSTRATE: *lying flat*
EFFICACIOUS: *effective*
ARDENTLY: *passionately*

CHAPTER VIII

IN THE CATACOMBS

THE little colony of Christians who had been driven to seek for new homes in a locality where they were least likely to find what they needed, owing to the havoc the river had made in that direction, had raised a few hovels of stones and mud, wood and thatch; but although they shared with each other all their earnings, and all that a few had managed to save from the general wreck around them, it was a hard struggle to keep famine at bay during the cold wintry days that followed closely upon the inundation.

Their neighbours, less poor and far less deserving, obtained frequent supplies of corn and meal from the imperial granaries; but viewed, as they were, as the cause of the prevailing distress, the poor Christians dared not make their wants known lest it should rouse the anger of their enemies against them into a more active display of violence than they had yet suffered. Insults and injuries they constantly had to endure; but these early followers of Christ took the import of the

Divine word literally, and when they were struck "on one cheek turned the other also,"[1] believing that the manifestation of their true dignity, as sons and daughters of the Lord God Almighty was close at hand, when they would be exalted and their enemies confounded. Such marvelous meekness under wrongs unjustly inflicted only exasperated some, but others were so overcome by it that they sought to know more of this religion that could bring forth such fruit. So it sometimes happened that not only wool carders and tufa diggers, but one and another from the wealthy patrician families of Rome crept to their little church underground, to learn something of the wonderful love of Christ dying to redeem them.

Winter passed away at last, but sickness came with the warm spring days, and one of the first attacked was the fair-haired girl of Plautius, the vinedresser. The child had not been strong since they left their cottage in the valley, and a few days' sickness carried her home to the land where there is neither sorrow nor sickness. Plautius tried to subdue his grief, as became a Christian; he did not talk of throwing himself into the Tiber or blame anyone for the death of his child, as one of his fellow-labourers was doing at the same time, but he did not love her less; he felt his loss most keenly, but he had the hope of meeting his beloved child again: a hope that was laughed at and derided when he ventured to mention it to his comrade while they were at work, for, whatever their grief

---

[1] MATTHEW 5:39

DERIDED: *mocked*

might be, they must go to work still. And as they dug out the tufa side by side they each decided to smooth and level the niche on which they were working, and, as it would not be dug any farther in that direction, to lay the remains of their children there, one in each, and over each they would place some mark. Plautius was not a learned man, and could neither read nor write; and so he had to content himself with cutting a representation of a vine, with one bunch of grapes severed from the parent stem. The idea of thus distinguishing his daughter's grave was by no means original. A shoemaker had been buried a short time before, and his friends had cut the likeness of a pair of slippers, by way of epitaph, and more than one of those engaged in digging had chosen the niche for their own grave, and cut the images of their tools upon the stone above.

The companion in sorrow of Plautius, however, could boast of having received a liberal education in his youth, and so he set to work to cut not only the name of his son, but a long tirade against the gods who had deprived him of his presence. "Cruel and relentless, ye have snatched him from a father's side, to plunge him in the darkness of the land of shades, where I shall never see him more." This was how the epitaph concluded, and Plautius might well pity the despairing heart of the father who could write such bitter words as these. Seeing, however, that his fellow-workman could write, Plautius resolved to ask him to make an addition

EPITAPH: *an inscription in memory of someone*

to his inscription by placing underneath these words: "She rests in peace."

The man stared when asked to place these words above a grave. "In peace at rest?" he asked.

"Yes, she rests in Christ, and is at peace," replied Plautius; "and whenever I pass this way I shall love to think that my Julia sleeps in the grave my own hands dug."

"I shall never come here to work again after my son is laid here," said the sorrow-stricken father. "I must forget I ever had a son, or I shall curse the gods that I did not die with him," he continued, and hurried away before a word of comfort could be spoken.

Little Julia was laid to rest one bright spring day, and the following week her brother was laid beside her; and at the same time the minister of the Church and his wife were borne to their last resting-place by the members of their sorrowful flock. These were laid near the entrance of the church, and above was cut a phonetic sign that might well puzzle the uninitiated, but would tell of faith, and hope, and joy to every Christian who should pass that way. A circle was first drawn, to represent eternity. Inside this were the Greek letters X and P, combined into a cross,  and on either side were the letters Alpha and

Omega, the first and last of the alphabet. In these signs the initiated would perceive the initials of the name of their Lord, the instrument of His atoning death, and the declaration that He was from eternity to eternity. The rude picture of a fish was added, the letters of its name, in Greek, being the initials of the words  *Jesus Christ, Son of God, Saviour.*

This, therefore, was what they could read in the sign of the circle with its hieroglyphics, "Jesus Christ, God's Son, the Saviour, died on the cross, yet lives throughout eternity, for He is the first and the last, the beginning and the end."

The hearts of these poor Christians sorely needed all the comfort their faith could give them, for there was scarcely a family where death had not entered. When, therefore, the time for their usual *agape*, or love-feast, came round, many looked forward to it as a season of soul-refreshing strength and comfort. Only those who had been admitted into the Church by baptism were permitted to partake of this, as in the case of the Lord's Supper, which it not infrequently followed. It was scarcely a "feast," in the modern sense of that word, for it was never other than a frugal meal, usually of bread, wine, and a dish of herbs, which were spread on a small table in the center, and around which, but some distance away, sat the guests, the men on one side, the women on the other. Following literally the apostolic injunction, they greeted each other with the kiss of charity on entering, and as soon as all were assembled prayer was offered, a hymn sung, and then, while they partook of the meal, matters relating to the Church were discussed freely.

It was not strange that at this spring *agape* the subject of discussion should be the resurrection, and out of this grew the memorable visit of Polycarp, Bishop of Smyrna, who had traveled to Rome a few years previously to confer with the bishop, Anicetus, upon the subject of keeping the paschal feast. John, the beloved disciple, and Polycarp's teacher, had always observed the Jewish rule regarding this day, and, counting the fourteenth day of the moon after the spring equinox, had kept this in memory of the great sacrifice of the Lamb of God, and the third day from that as the resurrection, without regard to the day of the week on which they might happen to fall. In this he had been followed by all the Churches in the East. But those of Rome, Carthage, and Alexandria preferred to keep the original day on which the Lord had died, and so they observed the Friday for this, and the following Sunday for the resurrection.

Their present bishop, Victor, was a presbyter at the time of Polycarp's visit, and he related how the venerable old man, who was now almost the last living link between their days and that

PASCHAL: *Passover*
PRESBYTER: *elder*

of the first disciples, had come in leaning on his staff, and how, as his senior and superior, Anicetus had deferred to him, although they could not agree upon the matter which had brought him to Rome, and therefore had wisely determined that if they could not see eye to eye upon this question of minor import it should not interfere with the weightier matters which were dear to the heart of each. Anicetus, as Bishop of Rome, had the largest Church, but he had no thought of arrogating to himself any superiority on that account, but rather looked upon the Bishop of Smyrna as his superior, though Polycarp would have deprecated this as savouring too much of a desire to lord it over God's heritage.

"I love to think that the hands which often grasped those of the beloved John once clasped mine, and that I received from them the bread and wine in memory of the Lord's death, which his teacher first ate with the Lord Himself," said Victor, as he concluded his account.

Many of those sitting there had heard of Polycarp's visit before, and some had been present at the time; but to Plautius and his wife it was quite new. It appeared to cast an afterglow upon that time, which seemed to have receded so far back, when the Lord Himself walked this earth, and talked with them.

"Does Polycarp still live?" the vinedresser asked of his neighbour.

ARROGATING: *presumptuously claiming*
DEPRECATED: *disapproved of*

"Yes, he was alive and well the last time we had tidings from Smyrna," answered the man.

"I should greatly like to see him," said Plautius. "My wife has a sister who has gone to Smyrna. She was a slave here in Rome, but her master was offended because she was a Christian, and sold her out of his family;" and he sighed as he thought how much Nerissa could comfort his wife if she were here now.

When the meal was concluded the parchment scroll presented to them by Polycarp, containing the three epistles of his beloved teacher, John, was brought from its hiding-place, and a portion of it was read. Then they again united in prayer, after which a hymn was sung, the kiss of peace was exchanged, and tenderly embracing each other as brethren they departed to their own homes.

Plautius soon began to fear that his wife would follow her children to the grave, and though this would be a gain to her it would be an almost irreparable loss to himself, and at length he decided to return to their former home if possible. The little vineyard he had cultivated might be restored, he thought; and he set off on his walk to Aricia the next day, to see about this. But here an unforeseen difficulty awaited him. His former neighbours and the owner of his little piece of ground had heard of his joining the Christian Church, and the landlord refused to let him have the ground again, while the neighbours declared that they would not live near him, lest some fresh calamity should befall them through his atheism.

Sadly disappointed and disheartened, Plautius returned to his wife, wondering where they could go, for if the lives of herself and her youngest child were to be saved they must leave Rome very soon. To his surprise, his wife did not seem so disappointed at the failure of his errand as he thought she would be. "The Lord is working for the best," she said, quietly; and the next minute she added, "I should greatly like to go to Nerissa."

"But Nerissa is at Smyrna," said her husband.

"Could we not go to Smyrna to her?" asked his wife. She had no idea of the distance it was from Rome, and Plautius only had a dim understanding that it was beyond Ostia, the great seaport of Italy, and, therefore, somewhere beyond the sea. But although he smiled at his wife's suggestion he made inquiries among his friends about the climate and soil of the distant place, and whether his knowledge of vinedressing would be likely to prove useful there. What he heard concerning this matter so delighted him that he resolved to go to Ostia and try to make some terms with a shipmaster to take them to Smyrna as soon as possible; though what his wife would say to the prospect of a sea-voyage he did not know. He would tell her first that this must be undertaken. "I am sure of employment as a vinedresser there," he said; "for the soil is so fertile and the climate so warm that the vines yield two crops a year, and figs and spices grow in abundance."

"And we shall see Nerissa, and the great Bishop Polycarp, who came here a few years since," said his wife cheerfully. But the next minute the smile faded from her pale, worn face, and she said slowly, "I want to see Nerissa, but oh, Plautius, I cannot go away from Rome—away from the Catacombs where my little Julia and Marcinius are buried;" and the poor woman burst into tears.

"Hush, hush, my beloved, our little ones are not in the Catacombs, and we shall be as near them in Smyrna as in Rome," said Plautius, gently soothing her. "For the sake of the one lamb yet left to us we must go away from here," he added; "and at Smyrna I am sure to find employment, even if I cannot get a piece of ground to cultivate myself."

Julia looked at the child on her knee, so pale and sickly. Perhaps the sea-breezes and a change of climate would restore roundness to those little shrunken arms, and bring back the faded colour to his cheeks. For his sake she would try to overcome her yearning to stay near the resting-place of her sleeping darlings, and, trusting their bodies as she had trusted their souls in the hands of their Father and hers, would go in search of health and strength for the one still left in her care. So she agreed to her husband's proposal and promised to prepare for their voyage at once, so that if he could find a shipmaster willing to take them for the small sum of money they could afford to pay, there might be as little delay as possible in their departure, for now that her mind was made up to go away she was anxious to do so at once.

Plautius was more successful at Ostia than he had been at Aricia. The first shipmaster he applied to agreed to take him and his wife if he would make himself useful while on the voyage, and this he was quite willing to do. So the bargain was completed at once, and soon afterward they took an affectionate farewell of the friends who had been as loving brothers and sisters to them for the last few months, helping them in their distress, and consoling them in sorrow. With one or two who were going with them as far as Ostia they departed from the Imperial City, and in a few hours were sailing out on the mighty deep.

CHAPTER IX

AT EPHESUS

THE wish Flaminius so strongly expressed to leave Rome, if possible, Marcus Aurelius soon found an opportunity of gratifying, for a vacancy occurred in the provincial government of Ephesus, and the vacant post was offered to Flaminius, who most readily accepted it. The spring of the year was most favourable for such a voyage as must now be undertaken, and Flaminius was not the only one leaving Rome for the Panormus, for many of the wealthy Romans, weary of the gaieties of the Imperial City, blended the pursuit of pleasure with a sort of religious pilgrimage by attending the festival of Diana, or Artemis, which was continued through the whole month of May. It was called "Artemisius," or the month of Artemis, in Ephesus, when the city was so full of strangers —pilgrims and pleasure-seekers—that tents were often pitched outside the city walls for the entertainment of those who could not find any other accommodation.

The city, therefore, presented a very gay and animated appearance when Flaminius, with his family and household of five hundred slaves, arrived; for it was about the middle of the festival, and the citizens could think of nothing, talk of nothing, but their great goddess, and the games and shows now exhibiting in her honour. If Flaminius had not been a person of some consequence he would have been treated with scant ceremony by the mixed crowd in the street; but the slaves of the governor had been sent to escort his chariot and litters from the harbour to the house prepared for him, and so they met with but little annoyance from the mob.

Flavia, whose health had been quite restored by the sea voyage, raised the curtains of her litter and gazed upon the motley crowd hurrying to the temple or the gymnasia beyond the gates, while all the shops or booths were filled with little shrines or models of the magnificent temple for which the city was famed. The lady sighed heavily, and turning to her sister she said, "Ephesus, like our Rome, is wholly given to idolatry."

Sisidona's cheeks flushed. "How knowest thou that I deem the worship of the gods idolatry?" she asked.

"Nay, my sister, I wish not to force thy confidence; but thou didst tell me ere we left Rome that thy faith in them was broken."

Sisidona turned aside her head. "Do not heed

MOTLEY: *greatly varied*
GYMNASIA: *athletic school*

anything I may say," she exclaimed, impatiently. "I sometimes wish there were no gods in whom either to believe or disbelieve, and then there would not be all this painful doubt and uncertainty as to which should be worshiped."

"There is no doubt, there is no uncertainty, my sister," said Flavia, quickly, laying her hand tenderly on Sisidona.

But the young lady threw it off petulantly.

"Thou art forgetting I have promised never to discuss these things with thee," she said. "Thou wouldst not promise, I know, Flavia; but I did, and I must keep my promise. I cannot altogether control my thoughts," she added, "and I know thou dost often surmise what is passing in my mind; but I must not—dare not—talk about it; I want to forget it if I can."

Flavia looked into her sister's restless, dissatisfied face. "Thou art not happy, Sisidona, I can see," she said. "I may not talk to thee, thou sayest, but I can pray for thee, and that will be a greater help than any words I can speak."

Sisidona did not reply, and nothing more was said until the litters were set down at the door of the mansion which was to be their future home.

A troop of slaves had accompanied them, but the main body, with the chests of clothes and various articles of furniture, and the images of their ancestors, brought from Rome, were left at the harbour for the present. Flavia's first care was to

PETULANTLY: *irritably*

examine the rooms of the house, and select the most airy and cheerful for her children, and after seeing them settled here with their slaves, she selected rooms for herself, her husband, and sister, so that no one should suffer any discomfort or inconvenience. A visit paid some time later to the rooms occupied by the slaves revealed many things that needed alteration, and she at once begged her husband to have it done.

Flaminius smiled at the earnestness with which she preferred her request. "Have the lazy, fastidious rogues been complaining to thee?" he asked, "or art thou not content with wearing thyself out for the children, but must take up thy slaves to care for?"

"We ought to care for them!" answered Flavia.

Her husband laughed. "Whoever heard of such a thing?" he said. "All that is required of us is that we are not needlessly cruel to them."

"That is the teaching of the demi-gods; but with the true God it is not so. In His sight all men are free and equal, and there are but two classes—the sheep and the goats—those who believe in and love the Lord Christ, and those who despise His name," said Flavia, speaking with almost trembling earnestness.

Her husband rose from his seat and pushed her aside, but the next minute he came back and looked tenderly into her tearful face. "I do not believe in thy God, Flavia, but I believe in thee," he

PREFERRED: *presented*
FASTIDIOUS: *excessively delicate*
DEMI-GODS: *half-gods*

said, "and this must satisfy thee. I will not try to interfere with thy religion again; and if I leave thee to follow thy will in this matter, thou must leave me to follow mine," saying which he hastily left the room. It was the first time the matter had been spoken of since her illness; and Flavia felt both relieved and distressed—relieved, that her husband had relented thus far, and had no intention of leaving her or removing the children again, but at the same time distressed that she was forbidden to mention the subject that was dearest to her heart; for she had indulged the hope lately that her husband and sister were not altogether indifferent to what had become a matter of vital importance to her.

Whatever the private feelings of Flaminius might be he seemed determined to keep a watchful eye upon his sister-in-law; for, almost immediately after their arrival, he proposed that they should go to the Temple of Artemis and sacrifice, and afterwards witness the exhibition of the great goddess, for the sacred statue enshrined in this peerless Temple of Ephesus was only to be seen during this festival. A curtain depending from the ceiling was then solemnly drawn aside for a short time, that pilgrims might gaze on the great image of their goddess that fell from heaven.

Among those who pressed toward the temple the next day were Flaminius and Sisidona, attended by slaves, as became their rank.

PEERLESS: *without equal*
DEPENDING: *hanging*

The streets were thronged with gay and elegant chariots and litters, which could scarcely make their way through the motley crowd, some of whom dressed in fancy costume, as gods and goddesses: Jupiters with towering, glittering crowns, bolts of war, and white sandals; or Apollos in wreaths and white robes; eager pleasure-seekers, on their way to the theater with its shows, the hippodrome with its horse-racing, or the stadium with its wrestling and beast-fighting; and some, like Flaminius and Sisidona, making their way to the temple—pilgrims from all parts of Europe and Asia—desirous of seeing the great goddess once in their lives.

The Temple of Diana was the wonder of the world for beauty and magnificence. It was 425 feet long, 220 feet wide, and was 220 years in building. The glittering marble edifice could be seen for miles around, both by sea and land, and so there was no difficulty in finding the way to it; and when at length Sisidona descended from her litter she might well stand spell-bound in blank amazement, for, accustomed as her eyes were to grandeur and beauty, this temple of the huntress-queen surpassed anything of which Rome could boast. The whole temple was centered round a small cell, within which was the shrine of the goddess. Round this were colonnades of pillars, each 60 feet in height, of a single shaft of marble, jasper, and porphyry, each given by a king, for all the cit-

HIPPODROME: *an arena for horse racing*
PORPHYRY: *purple rock from a particular Egyptian quarry*
APELLES: *a famous painter in ancient Greece*

ies in Asia had united in the building of this glorious temple. There were 127 pillars arranged in an
oblong form, making a double row open to the sky.
Within these was the temple itself; its doors and
roof of cedar wood, while within were gathered
trophies of art such as the world has never since
seen equalled. A picture by Apelles, represent-
ing Alexander the Great grasping a thunderbolt,
hung on one side. The magnificent altar of Parian marble was from the chisel of Praxiteles, while
gold and jewels were lavished in richest profusion.
Warriors hung their trophies here, while men of
peace brought votive offerings or erected golden
statues. Before this shrine altars always smoked,
and the air was laden with richest perfumes.

Flaminius and Sisidona had not come empty-
handed; but their richest gifts seemed poor beside
the wealth, magnificence, and beauty scattered all
around; but they cast their incense into the flame,
watched the costly spices slowly pass off in smoke,
and then prepared to enter the temple itself to
see this wonderful image of the goddess; for if the
temple and all its surroundings and appointments
were so magnificent, what must be the beauty of
the deity who presided over all?

Sisidona would have preferred paying another
visit to see this crowning glory.

"I have seen enough for today," she whispered
to Flaminius. "When the curtain is drawn aside,
and the huntress-queen herself is disclosed to our

PARIAN MARBLE: *marble from the island of Paros*
PRAXITELES: *a famous sculptor in ancient Greece*
VOTIVE OFFERINGS: *offerings of devotion*

view, I want to be able to worship her at once—instinctively—I want her marvelous beauty to *compel* my adoration, so that I may never wander in my allegiance to her again."

Flaminius smiled. "Her beauty will not overpower thee," he said, significantly.

Sisidona, however, did not notice this.

"I do not want to be overpowered, but convinced," she said.

"Convinced that this is the great Diana of the Ephesians, whose image fell from Jupiter?" inquired Flaminius. "There is little doubt about it, Sisidona," he added; "but thou must see it today, or wait until next year;" and they pressed forward so as to obtain a good view of this marvelous image. What would it be like? Would the calm, stately queen be crowned with the crescent moon, a quiver at her back, the bow in her hand, and the fawn at her side, the whole executed in the finest gold or ivory, with an art rivaling that of Praxiteles? This was what Sisidona was prepared to see. But when at length the magnificent curtain was drawn aside, she almost screamed with horror at the sight of what it disclosed. A little rude lump of black stone, the part from the waist downward not shaped at all, and the upper part merely carved out into a head, a pair of arms, and roughly-cut breast. Anything uglier could not be well-imagined, and Sisidona experienced such a revulsion of feeling that if it had not been for the crowd, and the detaining arm of her brother-in-law, she would have rushed from the place.

Flaminius pointed out to her the mysterious letters carved on the clumsy feet, and commented on the gorgeousness of her apparel, and the peculiar signs on her crown and girdle, which the Ephesians regarded with such reverential awe, that copies of them, written on parchment, were worn as charms. But Sisidona saw nothing of this costly splendour; the goddess herself, in her revolting ugliness, was all she could see, and even the beauty of the temple was forgotten in the disappointment she felt at this. On their way home Flaminius purchased a little silver shrine or model of the famous temple, for these could be bought in gold, silver, or wood, and formed quite a profitable business. All visiting the city wished to take back to their homes a memento of its far-famed temple; and Flaminius, though he hoped to spend many years of his life at Ephesus, thought he would take one of these to his children, as a memento of this his first visit to the guardian deity of the place. Perhaps, too, he was anxious to screen his wife's opinions from comment, by showing that the popular goddess was worshiped in his household. He had no wish to hear her called a Christian here, as she had been at Rome, and so he was most desirous that Sisidona should pay all possible respect to the gods, hoping by this means to conceal Flavia's remissness.

But Sisidona was very indifferent about this matter. Sometimes it was too much trouble to go to the temple, or she had an engagement at the hippodrome, for she had suddenly grown very fond of pleasure and excitement—so fond, indeed, that Flaminius thought it his duty, as her guardian, to remonstrate on the extravagance into which she was rushing; for as the ancient law of Rome forbade a man to leave his wealth to a woman, Flaminius had inherited the property of his wife and her sister, but with the distinct promise that he held it in trust for their benefit, a trust that was never broken on his part.

He therefore ventured to remind Sisidona that she had been entrusted to his care, not only by her father, but by her betrothed husband, Claudius Rufus; for Claudius had been sent into Gaul just before they left Rome, otherwise they would have been married, for the emperor's consent had already been obtained. Flaminius wished that his friend would return now, and relieve him of the onerous charge, and he said as much to Sisidona. But the young lady tossed her head and pouted.

"Thou art hard to please, Flaminius," she said. "I must not talk to Flavia, for fear I should become like her, and I may not go to the theater or stadium, or—"

"Stop, Sisidona," commanded Flaminius; "when did I say I did not wish thee to be like thy sister?

REMONSTRATE: *express disapproval*
ONEROUS: *difficult, unpleasant*

If thou wert like Flavia I should have no reason to complain."

"But Flavia is a Christian," said Sisidona, provokingly.

"Thou needest not remind me of that fact," answered Flaminius. "I do not wish thee to forsake the gods of Rome—I do not ask thee to believe in the strange God Flavia worships—I only—"

"I don't believe in any god at all now," interrupted Sisidona, speaking very bitterly; and the next minute she burst into tears.

Flaminius was perplexed. "Hush, hush! I wish not to vex thee," he said, soothingly. "I have been harsh, perhaps, but I have much to try me here, much that I cannot tell Flavia, for fear of grieving her."

"Canst thou not tell me?" asked Sisidona, suddenly looking up and dashing the tears from her eyes.

"Well, there is a Church of these Christians here in Ephesus, and the terrible fire that took place a short time since is declared by the priest of Artemis to be caused by the anger of the gods against their innovators. The silversmiths are constantly making complaints, too, that their business is endangered by this new religion; and, to add to the complication, informers come every now and then proffering information against one and another who are known to be wealthy, merely for the sake of the reward they hope to obtain out of

INNOVATORS: *those who would change them*

the bribe the Christians will pay to be let alone."

"And what dost thou do—which side dost thou take?" demanded Sisidona.

"I can but state the law; I am not the proconsul," said Flaminius, evasively.

"And thou art unable to plead for or defend these poor people, and no one else in Ephesus will do it either. Flaminius, dost thou not think there must be some truth in a religion that can make people as brave as these Christians are?" she suddenly demanded.

Flaminius looked at her in silent astonishment for a minute or two, and then asked:

"What dost thou mean, Sisidona?"

"I mean that if there be a God at all, He is the God whom these Christians worship," she said, in a calm, measured tone; and without pausing to see the effect of her words she left the *peristyle* and went to her own chamber.

PROCONSUL: *governor of a province*

CHAPTER X

THE STORM THREATENING

FLAVIA sat in a darkened chamber beside her sister's couch. "Sisidona, dost thou know me?" she whispered tenderly, bending over the sick girl with a look of weariness and anxiety in her face that showed how long she had been watching there, battling for the life of the dear one she feared was passing away.

"Where am I?" asked Sisidona, in a weak voice. But the next minute she turned her face to the wall, saying, "I remember it all now; and I—I am an orphan, alone in the world."

"Nay, nay, my sister, not alone, for the Lord Christ is with thee," replied Flavia.

"I don't know enough of thy God to say that. I am almost a Christian, as Claudius reproached me with being; but there must be a difference, Flavia, for thou didst not rave, and throw thyself into a fever when Flaminius left—"

"Hush, hush!" hastily interrupted her sister; "speak not of that. The parting between husband

and wife none can know, save those who have endured it, and God, who gives strength to bear it."

"But thou hadst the strength to bear that, and
I can't bear my loss, for oh, Flavia, I do love Claudius still!"

"Dear little sister, the Lord Christ wants to bear
this trouble for thee," said Flavia, the tears stealing into her eyes as she placed her arm around the
invalid's neck, and drew her head down upon her
shoulder.

"I want to rest on something, as I am resting on
thee now," whispered Sisidona. "It has been such a
long struggle, and I am so weary. If this great image of Diana had only been beautiful—beautiful
enough to command my reverence and worship
at once—I think I could have rested upon her as
my special goddess; but when I saw how ugly she
was I felt repelled, and then I said those words to
Flaminius that caused all the trouble."

"But they were true. Thou dost not regret having chosen the Christians' God to be thy God?"
asked her sister, anxiously.

"I cannot believe in the gods of Rome, as Claudius demands I shall; but it seemeth to me I am
suffering as a Christian without a Christian's hope
and strength."

"God is our Refuge and Strength in every time
of trouble,"[1] said Flavia.

"Yes, but I am not sure that He is my God," said
Sisidona, anxiously.

---

[1] PSALM 46:1

"But thou art His child, Sisidona. He created thee, and sent His Son to redeem thee from sin. Listen, my sister: 'Herein is love; not that we loved God, but that He loved us, and sent His Son to be the propitiation for our sins.'[1] Wilt thou not try to believe this, Sisidona? They are God's own words—His special message to thee to-day, and He wants thee to believe it and rest on Him."

"Flavia, if I could so rest—rest as I know thou dost—I think I could bear even this parting with Claudius more patiently than I do," whispered her sister.

"God will give thee patience as well as strength. Try to forget thyself entirely, and let the Lord Christ carry thee as I carry my little Flaminia over any rough place where she might trip or hurt her feet. This is a rough place in thy life-path, and thou art weak and weary, and cannot get over it thyself. The Lord Christ knows all this, Sisidona; but He can bear thee over it. And think, my sister, thou canst pray for Claudius that the Lord will make Himself known to him likewise."

Sisidona looked up into her sister's face: "Hast thou prayed for Flaminius?" she asked; and then added, "I know thou hast, Flavia, for thou dost believe in prayer; and yet he hates the Christians more than ever, and thought it his duty to inform Claudius that I was in danger of becoming one of them."

[1] I JOHN 4:10

Flavia coloured. "My dear husband!" she exclaimed, tenderly. "Thou knowest, Sisidona, that he acted from a sense of duty when he wrote to Claudius. He does hate our faith, I know: the great missionary apostle did the same at first; but he learned to love it afterward; and my Flaminius will be brought to a knowledge of the truth, I doubt not. I must pray, but God alone can work in his heart, and He knows the most fitting time for that."

"But, Flavia, I want Claudius to learn to love this truth which I have begun to seek; and then—then—that we may be united," she whispered softly. "Am I very selfish?" she added.

"Nay, my sister, it is but a natural wish," replied Flavia; "but I would have thee try and leave the matter in God's hands. Pray for Claudius if thou wilt, but let God choose how and when the answer shall come. He will know just what is best for both of you. And now thou must try to rest body and mind, or thou wilt have another relapse. I will have thy slave to watch beside thee now, for Flaminius wished to have some converse with me when he returned from the Forum today, and he will be awaiting me in the *peristyle*."

Flaminius and his family had been some months at Ephesus—months of anxiety they had proved, for war had followed close upon the heels of fire and famine to distress the empire yet more, and each in turn had been charged to the poor Christians as the cause. The proconsul knew not what

CONVERSE: *conversation*

to do, for the priests and augurs of their great goddess were continually publishing pretended messages from her against these people, and there had been more than one uproar in the marketplace, the people shouting, "Great is Artemis of the Ephesians," until they were threatened by the Roman soldiers, who could only restore quiet by clearing the great market of Jews, priests, and workmen, who were the chief instigators of the riot.

But both the proconsul himself and Flaminius began to feel that some steps would have to be taken to pacify the people, or there would be complaints sent to Rome of all these riots; and the only thing that could be done was to institute proceedings against the Christians for insulting the popular gods. Slowly this conviction had grown into a certainty, and now it had received confirmation, for the proconsul had ordered the arrest of three citizens who were known to have spoken against the temple and its presiding deity. Flaminius therefore might well be anxious, for he knew not but that his wife or Sisidona might be the next informed against; and to buy off one informer was only a signal for others to spring up, so that a fortune might be spent to no other purpose than postponing the evil day. Flaminius had seen this again and again; he might therefore be excused for looking anxious and troubled when he met his wife in the *peristyle* that day.

Flavia saw that something was troubling him, and dismissing the children with their slaves she begged him to tell her the cause of his anxiety. "Hast thou received tidings from Claudius Rufus?" she asked.

"Nay; the expected messenger has not arrived from Rome yet. This war with Parthia is doubtless occupying the emperor's attention."

"Does he lead his soldiers in person?" asked Flavia, thinking she could lead him to speak of his trouble in that way.

"Nay, his adopted brother, Lucius Verus, was given the whole management of warfare at the time of the emperor's accession.

"Then wherefore art thou so sad, my Flaminius?" asked Flavia, tenderly. "Is it the thought of this war?"

Her husband looked down into the fair, pale, gentle face, and smoothing back the bands of her soft brown hair, he said, "Flavia, suppose it is thee, and such as thee, who are bringing this calamity upon us—for this war is a calamity, following, as it does, upon the inundation and the famine," he added.

The lady raised her eyes questioningly. "What have I done to throw a whole province into war?" she asked, in a tone of astonishment.

"Dost thou not know, my Flavia, or must I tell thee what the mob were crying again yesterday?"

"Oh, Flaminius, there has not been another riot?" she asked, with whitening lips.

"There was not a riot, because the proconsul promised to silence those who reviled the gods of Rome and Ephesus."

"Are the Christians to be persecuted?" she asked, in a faint whisper of suppressed agony.

"They must sacrifice to Diana, or be thrown into prison, and their property confiscated," replied Flaminius, sadly. His wife knew what he was thinking of; but how could she assure him she would not bring this trouble and disgrace upon their home, when to do this she must deny her Lord and Master?

Lower and lower drooped her head as she stood silently by his side, and the tears fell upon the marble pavement one after another in quick succession. Neither spoke for some minutes; but at length Flaminius said, "Flavia, thou knowest my thoughts upon this matter, but I promised never to interfere again with thy strange faith, and I will keep my promise." She did not need to be reminded that a promise was to Flaminius as sacred as the most solemn oath or binding contract. He had all the old Roman reverence for truth, and his word once passed would never be falsified.

For some minutes she could not speak, but at last she managed to say:

"Oh, my Flaminius! if thou wert but one of us I could go to prison or to death cheerfully, but this—this is the agony of persecution, that it separates husbands and wives, and plunges a sword

into many hearts sharper than that of the gladiator or cruel soldier."

Her husband made no reply, but after another
pause he said, "Wilt thou tell me what I am to say,
if I am asked whether thou wilt sacrifice to the
gods?"

"Oh, Flaminius, spare me!" pleaded Flavia.

He passed his arm around her waist to keep
her from falling to the ground, for her agitation
seemed to deprive her of all her strength. "I have
not been the cause of this persecution," he said,
as calmly as he could speak; "but now that it is begun, we know not when it may end, or who may be
the next accused. I cannot spare thee, my wife; the
decision must rest with thyself."

"I cannot deny the Lord who bought me with
His own blood," replied Flavia, with trembling
earnestness.

"Is that thine answer, Flavia?" asked her husband, battling with the pain he felt, and trying to
steady his voice.

"It must be; oh, Flaminius, I must not, dare not
give thee any other!" she almost shrieked, in her
agony, for this was a trial for which she was wholly
unprepared. Fearing that the slaves would over-
hear words that might but hasten the calamity he
was anxious to avoid, Flaminius took his wife in
his arms and carried her to her own room, and
laying her on the couch he said:

"Now, Flavia, thou must calm thyself and listen
to me. For Sisidona's sake, for my sake, thou must

be careful where thou dost go, and what thou doest or sayest, even before our own slaves. It may be that this persecution will pass away without any accusation being brought against thee. I am known as a worshiper of the gods, and that may be sufficient to satisfy the citizens," he added.

"Oh, my Flaminius, if thou didst but know the God who is a Refuge and Strength in every time of trouble, I should not fear this persecution," said Flavia, earnestly.

"Thy wishes are useless," said her husband.

"But my prayers are not," said his wife, with a faint smile.

"If those prayers are answered, thy God must be powerful indeed, for I have not grown dissatisfied with Apollo and Diana, as Sisidona has," replied Flaminius; and then he made some inquiries about the invalid, and various domestic matters concerning the children and slaves; for, unlike most Roman matrons of her rank, Flavia had undertaken the oversight of her own household, and knew when her slaves were ill and unable to work, and whether a certain dish she might order for supper was likely to cost a few sesterces, or the tribute of a whole province, which was more than many ladies in Ephesus could say.

After her husband left her she lay pondering on what she had heard, and silently praying that she might, if possible, be spared this trial, not so much for her own sake as for her husband's. Her rank, she knew, would be no protection, for ladies of higher birth, and occupying a more exalted position than she did, had suffered banishment and death for embracing this "superstition." In the reign of the Emperor Domitian, his niece Domitilla, the wife of a consul, was banished, and her husband put to death, so that it was scarcely likely that Flavia would escape if it were once publicly known that she was a Christian. Many of her own household slaves were aware of this, but Flavia thought they might be trusted; and so, after committing her cause to God in prayer, she endeavoured to dismiss her fears and anxieties for the present, lest she should be unfitted for the duty of nursing Sisidona, and doing what she could to lighten her husband's cares. There would also be another duty devolving upon her if this persecution should be commenced. She had joined the Church at Ephesus, and was one of the few wealthy and influential members. Now, if any of the poorer brethren were cast into prison their families must be cared for while they were there, and it was the duty of the wealthy thus to bear part, at least, of their burdens, and so fulfill the law of Christ, and prove that the lessons of their former bishop, the "Apostle of Love," were not yet forgotten.

As Flavia went back to her sister's clamber she tried to recall the picture of that feeble, yet mighty, old man, being borne through the streets in his litter; pausing every now and then, when his friends pressed around him, to breathe the well-known

DEVOLVING: *falling*

benediction and command, "Little children, love one another." These Ephesian Christians were his own flock, his "little children," whom he had led and taught for many years. He was taken from their midst, and hurried before the Emperor Domitian, accused of having ruined the worship of Artemis, and from thence to the lonely Isle of Patmos, where the Lord talked with His faithful and beloved disciple, once more revealing to him things yet to come upon the earth. His flock wept and mourned the loss of their leader, fearing they should never see his face again; but, after the death of Domitian, John returned from exile, and lived many years. All this Flavia had heard from Christian friends, some of whom could remember the white-haired old man, who usually carried a tame partridge nestling in his bosom, and whom no one was afraid to approach. She wished she, too, had been privileged to meet him, but she checked the thought almost as it arose, for had she not his Master, to whom she could go with every trial and difficulty, however peculiar or unforeseen it might be?

CHAPTER XI

AT SMYRNA

PLAUTIUS, the vinedresser, was warmly welcomed by his fellow-Christians at Smyrna. This bond of love to God and love to each other was no slight one in those days. Difference of nationality and even of language did but intensify this principle of unity and brotherhood where men were at one in religious aims and hopes; for religion was no outside affair, to be put on and off at will, like a garment, but was regarded as the chief object in life, to which all others were subservient.

So when Plautius, with his delicate wife and sickly child, reached the "City of Myrrh," a welcome awaited him as warm as that which had been given to him when he moved from Aricia into the Imperial City; for the brethren of Smyrna were not forgetful of the apostle's exhortation to "entertain strangers,"[1] and so this stranger from Rome was received as a brother in Christ.

When their bishop, Polycarp, heard of his arrival he made special inquiry for those whom he

---

[1] HEBREWS 13:2

remembered by name, as well as for the Church of Rome in general, and recommended Plautius to a wealthy citizen who owned several vineyards on the slopes of the hills outside the city walls.

Smyrna nestled at the foot of a range of sheltering hills that shut out the cold northeast winds, and thus protected vineyards and olive-gardens, fig-orchards and spice-trees, flourished. Its inhabitants, conscious of their indebtedness to nature for the fruitfulness of the soil, but ignorant of nature's God, had personified "the great mother" in an idol called Rhea, who, with Dionysus (or Bacchus, as he was variously termed), the god of wine, was specially worshiped at Smyrna. She was said to have revivified him after he had been cut to pieces and placed in a caldron. This was, of course, a rude allegory of the power of nature; but the worship of this goddess, as well as that of Dionysus, was horrible, and called into exercise the worst passions of mankind. These orgies and mad revels were just concluding when Plautius reached the city, and it was not greatly to be wondered at that every second or third person he met on the way should be reeling with intoxication, for the chief priest had just received his crown, and Dionysus demanded that everyone should drown his senses in wine in his honour.

Looking upon a party of mad revelers as they were passing the temple dedicated to the Emperor Tiberius, and remembering how often he had joined in a similar worship of Bacchus,

REVIVIFIED HIM: *brought him back to life*

the vinedresser turned to the young man walking with him and said, "Will these ever rush into such folly and excess? Will the worship of Bacchus never come to an end?"

Fortunately for Plautius he spoke in the Latin tongue, while most of those living at Smyrna understood Greek only, or some serious trouble might have fallen upon him for the indiscreet speech.

His companion, Germanicus, feared at one time that some of the crowd understood what had been said as well as he himself did, for they were almost instantly surrounded by the crazy revelers, who danced and sang, and waved their vine garlands and wreaths around the little party of Roman strangers, until the baby screamed with fright at their wild antics, and Julia herself became alarmed lest she should be snatched from her husband's side and whirled away by one of the revelers. Germanicus, too, was scarcely less frightened, lest his impulsive countryman should say or do something that would betray who they were, and that they hated such revelings.

At length, to his great relief, something else in the street attracted their attention, and they ran off, leaving the little party of Christians to pursue their way to the gate in peace. Plautius wanted to see the mode of cultivating the vines here at once, but Gemanicus told him that many of the vineyards nearest the city would be almost stripped;

EVER: *always*

PLAUTIUS' RECEPTION AT SMYRNA

and so it proved, for the roads were scattered with the trailing branches in every direction; for here the festival had been held, and the priest crowned for the year. Germanicus told his fellow-countryman of this custom.

"Thy bishop, too, has been promised a crown by the Lord Jesus Christ Himself, has he not?" said Plautius. "I knew not that Smyrna awarded a crown to the priest of her god, but I heard that to Polycarp a special message had been sent by the mouth of his master and teacher, John, and that a crown had been promised to him, even a crown of life."

Germanicus smiled. "I am glad thou hast heard from the brethren at Rome something of our beloved bishop. He is indeed a worthy pupil of even such a man as John. But talk not much of his crown, for 'tis a sad matter for some to think of, inasmuch as he taketh the words to mean that a crown of martyrdom shall be given him at the last."

Plautius turned a shade paler. "Are the brethren persecuted here by the worshipers of these demons?" he asked.

"Could it be otherwise, seeing we run not to the same 'excess of riot' in this idol worship?"[1] asked Germanicus.

"Nay, but they accuse our brethren at Rome of going to greater lengths than themselves. They declare our holy mysteries of the *agape* and last supper to be more infamous than the Eleusinian

[1] I Peter 4:4

mysteries, because they are not permitted to be present who have not been baptized."

"But they suffer none to enter their mysteries but the initiated, wherefore then can they complain that we, too, have our mysteries? I know that vile accusations are brought against us; but we know that the worship of their Rhea and Dionysus is so vile that we dare not approach—dare not even be friends with those who practice such things; and thus, although we are still as poor as when John was in Patmos, few errors have crept in among us, for we have struggled to keep ourselves unspotted from the world."

"Ah! and it is a continual struggle to one who used to love these things," said Plautius, with something of a sigh.

Germanicus looked at him in surprise. "But surely thou hast never loved such rioting and reveling?" he said.

Plautius laid his hand on the young man's shoulder. "Were thy parents Christians before thee?" he asked.

"Yes; my mother could tell me of how she used to listen to John after he came from banishment, and my father had learned the same truth before he left Rome."

"Then thank God thou wert taught to love Him while thou wert young, for thou knowest not how hard it is to give up cherished sins and evil customs when thou hast lived half thy life in the practice of

them. I tell thee they are as hard to break as ropes
of vine withes, and bind thee just as tightly. Only
the breath of the Lord God Almighty can destroy
them at first, and that only can keep thee from
being bound again, for they are always trying to
creep over thee."

"Nay, but thou couldst not wish to join in such
wild revels as those we passed just now," said Germanicus.

"*Could not!*" repeated Plautius. "When the feast
of Bacchus was all I lived for, thinkest thou I did
not enjoy the rioting and drunkenness?"

"But thou couldst not enjoy it now?" said his
friend.

"I hope not, but I know not. I am often afraid of
myself lest the old love of this come over me; and
so thou seest it is still a struggle, and I would to
God idol-worship could be put down."

Plautius spoke the latter words almost passionately, and at the same moment a head appeared
on the other side of the myrtle-hedge near which
they were walking, and looked into the faces of
each.

Germanicus saw the look, and hoped the man
did not understand what had been said; but
whether he did or not he could not tell, for he did
not speak. He again gave Plautius a word of warning about needlessly exposing himself, not only
to insult but to possible danger by thus speaking
openly of his wish to destroy the worship of the

WITHES: *stems*

gods; and the vinedresser promised to be careful and discreet in this matter.

Julia would rather have gone in search of her sister than have come to look at the vineyards; but her husband had been so very anxious about this matter that she readily agreed to postpone making any inquiries about her until the following day. Some of those belonging to the Christian Church would be sure to know her, Plautius said, and Julia commenced her inquiries by asking Germanicus if he had heard of a Roman slave, Nerissa, being admitted to the Church.

The young man shook his head. "I do not say there is no such person in our Church of Smyrna, but I know her not," he replied.

"She has not been long in this city," said Julia; "canst thou not remember those who have come to thy Church lately?"

"Yes, we have not so many but I can remember them," answered their guide. "It may be she hath gone to one of our Churches outside the city."

"Nay, she would not do that, for she was anxious to be under the teaching of thy bishop, Polycarp; for, as he was once a slave himself, Nerissa said he could understand the troubles and sorrows of a slave better than any other," answered Julia, quickly; and she began to grow anxious about her sister, in spite of all her husband said to dispel her fears.

The next day, while he had gone upon the necessary business of obtaining employment, Julia went to make further inquiries about Nerissa; but no one had seen or heard anything of her. Certainly she had not joined the Church at Smyrna, which was a fact so startling that Julia began to fear she had not come to the "City of Myrrh" at all. With the exception of this disappointment, however, she had little cause to regret coming, for the baby grew stronger and more healthy every day, her own health was greatly improved, and once more among his vines, Plautius seemed to recover his cheerful and hopeful spirit. They had been installed in a little cottage on the edge of the vineyard of which Plautius had the charge, and here Julia could almost fancy she was again in the valley of Aricia, but for the absence of her children—the two who slept in the Catacombs of Rome—and that she never saw her sister as she did in the old days at home, as she loved to call her Italy.

Julia knew not what to think, what to do, to find her sister or discover her fate. Certainly she was not in Smyrna, for Plautius had made every inquiry, not only among the brethren in Smyrna, but at two little villages beyond, where there were small congregations of Christians, but no one had heard of Nerissa.

Anxiety about this, however, was soon absorbed in another that threatened to touch them even more closely than this. News of the Parthian War reached Smyrna in due time, and with it came an imperial edict for the imposition of a fresh tax to

EDICT: *proclamation*
IMPOSITION: *laying on*

support the troops in the East, which excited a great deal of complaint among the citizens. Their trade would be ruined by this tax, they grumbled, and it was hard that they should have to pay it, seeing that they had erected such a splendid temple to one of the Cæsars.

But the tax had to be paid, for the war was not over with the first blows that were struck; and the priests of Dionysus declared that it was useless to build temples to the emperor when they denied the very existence of the gods.

"Who had been guilty of such impiety? Who had dared to speak against the great mother Rhea and Dionysus, who gave them such abundant harvests?" asked one and another.

The priests of the goddess soon answered the question. "The Christians call our gods demons, and are constantly seeking to overthrow their worship."

"The Christians!" exclaimed the crowd of worshipers who were gathered round the steps of the temple. "Mean ye that miserable sect who drink not to the honour of our god, and are led in their impiety by the slave-bishop, Polycarp?"

"Even so," answered the priest. "These are the enemies of Smyrna—the enemies of the emperor, and who cause us to eat the bread of scarceness when our god would fain give us plenty."

"Polycarp to the beasts! We will have none of these Christians in Smyrna!" shouted two or three together; and they were about to leave the temple at once to go in search of Polycarp and drag him before the prefect. But one of their number, pitying the grey-haired old man whom he had often seen in the streets and marketplace, raised his voice above the rest and asked, "Which among ye heard Polycarp call our gods demons?"

There was a pause for a minute, while they looked in each others' faces asking the same question; for it would be useless to drag him before their prefect unless they could support this charge. At length one replied, "We know these Christians hate our gods, and a Roman vinedresser, who came here at our last festival, was heard to say that he hoped the worship of Dionysus would soon be overthrown."

"Then let the Roman be seized, but not Polycarp," said his defender.

It mattered little to the crowd whom they seized, so long as a victim could be found on whom they could wreak their vengeance; and the cry was instantly changed to "The Roman to the lion! Down with the Christians!" and, as though they were themselves the beasts thirsting for the blood of their victim, they rushed at once to the tribunal of the prefect, and demanded that this "superstition" should be suppressed, and the Christians destroyed. The prefect tried to pacify them with assurances that the honour of their gods should be maintained; that nothing could ever

TRIBUNAL: *court*

overthrow the worship of Jupiter and Rhea, and that the Christians' God would soon be forgotten, as He had neither temple nor statue in Smyrna. It was all in vain; and finding at length that a riot would ensue if he did not yield to their demands, he promised that the Roman vinedresser, who had insulted their gods, should be sought for and brought before him the next day, when they must produce their witnesses and such evidence as they had to bring against him. There was little difficulty in doing this. Only one man had really heard the incautious words of Plautius the day of his arrival; but half a dozen others were ready to swear that they, too, were present at the time, and heard what he said, and, as may be easily imagined, the original words had received several additions from each, so that the charge was no light one with these additions; and it seemed scarcely possible that Plautius could escape being doomed to the beasts at the next games, for his enemies knew well enough that he could not deny any of their intended charges without denying his religion; a thing that few ever expected, for the obstinacy of these Christians had almost passed into a byword.

BYWORD: *proverb*

CHAPTER XII

THE VICTIM

PLAUTIUS was on his way home, carefully noting the signs of the coming short winter, and thinking of his old home in Aricia, and how he had looked forward to each Bacchanalian festival with joyful expectation, when a hand was suddenly laid upon his shoulder, and on looking round he found himself face to face with the Roman guard sent to arrest him. To expostulate was useless; the men would not even allow him to go home and inform his wife of what had happened.

"She will hear it soon enough," said one of the men, roughly. "Thou wilt be brought before the prefect tomorrow morning, and some miserable Christian hound who will be in the crowd can go and tell her, if she be not sent for to answer for her crimes."

"What crimes?" asked Plautius. "We are honest, quiet citizens working for our daily bread and—"

"And bringing ruin on all the empire by thy superstition, and railing against the gods!" interrupted one of his captors, angrily. "I would rid the

EXPOSTULATE: *protest*
RAILING: *speaking harshly*

world of every atheist and Christian, if I were emperor."

"Come, come, we are wasting time," said the captain of the guard, as he examined the chain that had been attached to the prisoner's wrists; and the next minute they were marching back towards the gate of the city, while Plautius was thinking sadly of his wife's fear and anxiety through the lonely hours of the night. If Nerissa were only at hand, and could go to her, she would not be so lonely; but they had never heard of Nerissa, and so there was little to comfort and much to disquiet the poor man, as he sat in his gloomy dungeon, thinking of wife and child, and wondering what his punishment would be, for he knew the charge to be brought against him was that of railing against the gods.

Plautius was certainly startled with the overwhelming amount of evidence brought against him by the witnesses, each of whom affirmed that he had himself heard the prisoner call their gods demons, and wish that their worship might soon come to an end and themselves overthrown.

Certainly he had said as much, perhaps, to his own wife at home, and once he had been incautious enough to say something like this to his friend Germanicus, but it was when he first came, and then there was no one else near, and he had been careful not to do it since, so that it was impossible for all these people to have heard it as they

THE ARREST OF PLAUTIUS

asserted. The prefect heard the evidence, and then addressing the prisoner said there was a shorter way than listening to either his denial or affirmation of the charge. He could sacrifice at once to the goddess Rhea, and pour out a libation to their god Dionysus, and then he would be set at liberty.

Plautius glanced at the tripod from which the smoke of the incense went curling upward, and one of the attendants, thinking he was about to yield to the demands of the prefect, fetched the spices ready for him to throw on the sacred flame. But Plautius pushed it aside as it was handed to him.

"Thinkest thou I will deny the Lord who redeemed me from the service of these dumb idols?" he said.

"Swear by the godhead of the emperor, and thou shalt be free," said the prefect, anxious to save him if possible.

A murmur of dissatisfaction went through the crowd.

"The gods will shake our city with earthquake, even as they did Philadelphia long since, if these Christians are not put down," grumbled one in an audible whisper, and several others spoke in a similar manner.

The prefect might sneer at their gods in the privacy of his own chamber, but he scarcely dared to sneer at the expression of public opinion; and it was useful to pay some outward respect to the

TRIPOD: *a three-legged altar*

popular deities, whatever he might think of their power, for it gave him a greater hold upon the people, and helped him to govern them. So finding that Plautius would not swear by the emperor any more than he would sacrifice to the gods, he ordered him to be given over to the lictors to be scourged with their rods, and afterward taken back to prison. Meanwhile Julia had passed an anxious, sleepless night, watching for her husband's return. Early the next day she had taken her child to the vineyard in search of him, fearing that some accident had overtaken him, and she continued this search for several hours, wandering up and down every alley, and visiting every nook and corner.

Weary and anxious, not knowing which way to turn, or where to inquire for her husband, ignorant, as she was, of the language of the country, she had paused in the wood leading to the cottage when she saw the noble, venerable figure of their bishop, Polycarp, coming toward her. In a moment it flashed upon her that he was coming to see her, and, in spite of her anxiety for her husband, she hastened on to the cottage, opened the door, and placed a seat in readiness, for Polycarp was growing feeble, and was weary, she could see.

In a minute or two he came up to the door, and Julia invited him to come in and rest himself awhile.

"Art thou the wife of Plautius the vinedresser?" asked Polycarp.

"Yes," answered Julia, her heart sinking within her as she noticed the look of anxious concern on the gentle face of the bishop.

"Is—is my husband in trouble?" she asked, under her breath.

"My daughter, be of good cheer; the Lord hath stood by Plautius this day, and enabled him to witness a good confession before all men," said the bishop.

Julia started. "My husband—my husband!" she gasped; "is he—have they cast him to the lion?" her mind going back to that awful scene in the arena at Rome.

"Nay, nay! be comforted, my daughter. Plautius still lives, and may be with thee shortly," said Polycarp; and he took the child tenderly from her arms, and seated it on his knee.

"Forgive me," said Julia, as she burst into tears; "but I have grown over-anxious for my Plautius. Thou sayest he is coming speedily," she added, glancing out through the open door, in the hope that she might see him coming down the road.

"The Church will pray for his deliverance out of the hands of our enemies. He was taken before the prefect this morning, and charged with railing against the gods of Smyrna; but I doubt not he will be released from prison shortly," said the bishop.

Julia was not a heroine, but a poor weak woman, and for a few minutes nature triumphed over faith, and wringing her hands she cried: "Oh, my

Plautius, my Plautius! who will care for our babe, when thou art taken away? I am a stranger here, in a strange land."

"Nay, but thinkest thou that God is a stranger here? Dost thou forget His promises to the fatherless and widows, and thinkest thou that our brethren in Christ will forget thy necessities?" said Polycarp, quickly.

"Nay, think not of me, but of Plautius," sobbed Julia.

"The Church of Christ will care for both of you, and in proof of this I have come to bid thee welcome to the house of our deaconess until thy husband is released. She cannot speak the Latin tongue, it is true, but kindness can make itself understood without words, and of this thou wilt be certain with our sister."

He would not tell her of her husband's full punishment just now. By-and-by, perhaps, she would be better able to bear it; but the first shock was almost too much for her as it was. Many coveted the martyr's crown, but Julia was not one of these. She shrank from pain and suffering, both for herself and those dear to her, and now she could only take her babe in her arms and shed bitter tears over him as she thought of his father's probable fate.

Polycarp knew she would be better after her grief had had its way, and so he did not try to check her tears, but gently pointed her to the great Sufferer, who could sympathize with her fully and entirely,

DEACONESS: *a woman who serves in the church*

who would certainly be with her in her loneliness as well as with her husband in the prison.

But Julia shook her head sadly. "Nay, nay, but I dare not take such comfort to myself," she said, "I am so weak and faithless I would grudge my Plautius being sacrificed even for the name of the Lord Christ."

"But He who knows the heart of woman understands its weakness, and how to make it strong. He bids thee come to Him because thou art weak. Let us pray to Him even now, not only for Plautius, but for other of our brethren, who may be as sorely tried;" and Polycarp, raising his eyes to heaven, pleaded with God as one who spoke face to face with a friend.

When this was concluded he bade Julia gather what clothes she would need for herself and her child, and shutting the cottage door, they set off on their walk to Smyrna. On the way Julia told the bishop about her sister, and how disappointed she had been at not finding her in Smyrna. Polycarp, however, seemed to think she might be there, although they had failed to trace her. "Smyrna is a wealthy and luxurious place," he said. "Many of our citizens keep three or four hundred slaves, and if thy sister is waiting-maid to some fashionable lady she may not be able to join the Church of Christ here. The Lord hath many hidden ones, I doubt not, in this evil, licentious city," added the gentle bishop.

Julia was received with every demonstration of kindness by the deaconess, who was herself the widow of one who had suffered persecution, even unto death, in the reign of the Emperor Hadrian, and so she could sympathize with poor Julia, and managed to make her sympathy felt and understood, although she knew nothing of the language which her visitor spoke.

Polycarp did not stay long after he saw Julia comfortably settled and had himself rested, for, aged as he was, he had much to do just now. His flock must be encouraged to be brave and true to their Lord, should this threatened persecution become general. The Church had wisely forbidden anyone needlessly to expose their lives, or to give themselves up to the magistrates to be tried as Christians. If the trial of their faith came in the path of duty, then they must not deny their Lord; but to seek the crown of martyrdom as some surpassing glory was expressly forbidden. So Polycarp went to his flock to teach prudence and discretion as well as faith and hope, for many might be carried away at this time to speak not only against the dumb idols but against the rulers and magistrates; and so, although Polycarp spoke of the chains as "holy diadems of the truly elect of God," he yet exhorted them not only to pray for the saints and the Church of Christ, but said likewise, "Pray also for kings and potentates, and princes, and for those that persecute and hate you, and for the

DIADEMS: *jeweled crowns*
POTENTATES: *rulers*

enemies of the cross, that your fruit may be manifest to all."

These words had been written to the Philippians, when their aged bishop, Ignatius, had been taken from them, and suffered death in the arena at Rome; and he found it needful to exhort his own flock in a similar strain, for many were angry at the treatment of Plautius, and expressed it openly.

If the prefect thought to pacify the angry mob and the wily priests of Rhea with the sacrifice of one victim he was mistaken. The cry taken up against the Christians was not so easily quelled. The Jews were quite as hot and quite as fierce in their denunciations of these people, and many of the merchants of the city being Jews, the disquiet spread and increased until a riot was again threatened. Then came news of the disturbances at Ephesus, and that the proconsul had been obliged to commence a prosecution against the Christians in that city, and that many of them had sacrificed to the gods to escape further punishment.

This news was received with widely different feelings by the two parties now ranged against each other. To the Christians it was sadly disheartening, and Polycarp not only addressed a letter to their bishop, Onesimus, who, like himself, had tasted the bitterness of slavery when young; but special prayers were offered in the Church for their Ephesian brethren, that they might not only

QUELLED: *quieted*

be sound in the faith, rejecting the evil, sensual doctrine of the Nicolaitanes or Gnostics—who denied that Christ had suffered for the sins of the world, or that He was God's Son, as the Scriptures avowed; but that they might also be renewed and strengthened in faith and love.

To the Jews and the priests of the temples, who were now making common cause against the Christians, the tidings brought every encouragement to persevere in their demands, and accordingly a large crowd assembled before the prefect's house, and at once commenced their old cry, "The Christians to the lions, or Smyrna will be destroyed!"

Again the prefect yielded. What could he do? These turbulent Greeks must be kept quiet, if possible, or he would lose his post. Had they been nearer Rome the old national spirit might have been crushed entirely out of them by the legionaries of the emperor; but having little exercise in the way of lawful self-government, it sank into a brutal, lawless, furious demand, all the more fierce because this was the only outlet it could find, and it must be gratified at whatever cost.

This time Germanicus was seized and hurried off to prison, and for a time his persecutors were satisfied. It was a peace cheaply purchased, the prefect thought, for who esteemed these miserable, obstinate Christians? The sect would soon die out, and the very name of it be forgotten in a few years, he had no doubt; and so he went quite

self-complacently to take his daily bath, and discuss the size he should have his new fish-pond
made, while Germanicus and his companion in
bonds were encouraging themselves by prayer to
brave the fury of their enemies, and witness a good
confession before men if they should be called to
seal their testimony with their blood.

The vinedresser's chief anxiety had been removed by hearing that his wife and child had been
tenderly cared for by the Church during his imprisonment, so that he could now resign himself
more entirely to the will of God. Germanicus was
a young man who had no such close ties; but still
life, with its social joys, was dear to him, and he
could rejoice in the strength of a sound, temperate body until the lictors, with their cruel rods,
left him a mass of blood and bruises, to die or to
revive, without help or succour, after he had been
thrust into the miserable dungeon where Plautius
was still confined. Both prisoners felt it a great
mercy to be placed together, and Plautius, who
had endured the same suffering himself, did all he
could to alleviate that of his companion; but it depressed them both to think that this persecution
was likely to become general, for where or when it
would end none could tell, if it spread from city to
city, as it seemed likely to do.

SELF-COMPLACENTLY: *pleased with himself*
TEMPERATE: *restrained from indulgence*
SUCCOUR: *assistance in time of need*

CHAPTER XIII

AYASALUK

THE story that had reached Smyrna concerning the Christians of Ephesus had been greatly exaggerated, as such accounts generally are, but it was quite true that the Ephesians had greatly degenerated since the days when they had brought their books of "curious arts" concerning the charms to be wrought by the mysterious letters on the crown and girdle of their goddess, and burnt them in the sight of all men. The value of these books has been estimated at about £1,800[1] of our money, but they had learned to "count all things but loss for the excellency of the knowledge of Christ Jesus."[2] Little wonder was it that "so mightily grew the Word and prevailed,"[3] that many feared the temple of Artemis would be forsaken, and the trade of Ephesus ruined.

But these heroic days seemed to have passed away forever. Seventy years before this the Master had sent a message by the mouth of His servant John complaining, "Thou hast left thy first love.

---

[1] *Current value about £130,000 or $260,000*
[2] PHILIPPIANS 3:8   [3] ACTS 19:19-20

Remember, therefore, from whence thou art fallen, and repent, and do thy first works; or else I will come unto thee quickly, and will remove thy candlestick out of his place, except thou repent."[1]

Sadly had these words fallen from the lips of their apostle-bishop, John, and sadly were they repeated now by Onesimus; for if Ephesus had returned to her "first love" and done her "first works" Artemis would have had but few worshipers, and her midsummer fires would have long since been extinguished by the burning of those books of mysteries so nobly given up at the preaching of Paul.

But a time of trial had come to Ephesus, and while many, through fear of the consequences, conformed outwardly to the usages of her corrupt idolatrous society, others cheerfully endured persecution rather than deny their Lord and Master; while others, whom the world deemed happy and secure through the circumstances in which they were placed, suffered "a great fight of afflictions"[2] that no one knew of but He who strengthened them to endure it. Of this number was the noble Flavia. Each day she watched with growing concern the lines of care deepen on her husband's brow; and when she ventured to ask concerning his work at the Forum it was generally to hear that one or other of her Christian friends had publicly sacrificed to the gods, or been committed to prison; and she knew that Flaminius was living in

---

[1] REVELATION 2:5   [2] HEBREWS 10:32

daily, hourly terror lest she herself should be the next summoned before the proconsul. This it was, she knew, that made him look prematurely old and worn; this fear was undermining his health, and robbing him of all joy and pleasure in life; and yet she had to endure it, though it was a daily martyrdom more severe than stripes or imprisonment.

Often and often did the temptation come to her, when she heard of one and another sacrificing to the gods, to go herself to the temple of Artemis sometimes with other ladies of Ephesus. It would lift this load of trouble from her husband's heart, she knew, and they might be as happy and prosperous here as they had been at Rome. "No one will be any the worse, for you can pray to God in secret all the same," whispered the tempter again and again; but although Flavia suffered so keenly she would not listen to the plausible suggestion. Alone with God in her chamber, she fought the enemy, and conquered. Sisidona knew that her sister must be enduring a fierce struggle at this time, and one day she ventured to ask her why she did not follow the example of some of her friends, and pay a little outward respect to the gods when it would save so much anxiety and trouble.

Flavia was feeling very weary with the accumulated cares that were pressing upon her, but she shook her head decidedly.

"The Lord Jesus has redeemed me, and I must be loyal to Him—loyal unto the end," she added.

Sisidona looked into the pale, worn face. "Flavia," she said, "there are other martyrdoms than those which the world witnesses."

But her sister shook her head. "Nay, nay, I am no martyr," she said, quickly. "I can only just cling to the cross of the Lord Jesus and—"

"And help me to lay hold of it too," whispered Sisidona, interrupting her.

Flavia looked into the eyes that used to flash with such scorn when the name of Christ was mentioned, and saw there a look of tenderness—almost happiness. "My sister, thou dost love the Lord Christ?" she said, questioningly.

"I do not know. I cannot be sure of this wayward, passionate heart," said Sisidona, mournfully; "but I believe the Lord Christ loves me, unworthy as I am. Flavia, would He accept the love of such a torn, bruised heart as mine, when the best—the first love—was given to Claudius?" she asked.

"Yes, my Sisidona. He has specially invited such as thee, 'the weary and the heavy laden,'[1] those whom the world has beaten and buffeted with its storms, those who have sought rest and satisfaction in earthly love and pleasure, and found them cruelly deceptive, those who have tried every god in turn, and could not find one to suit their needs—to these He says, 'Come unto Me and rest.'"

[1] MATTHEW 11:28

"And thou canst rest, Flavia, or thou couldst not bear all thou hast," said Sisidona.

"Yes! He who has borne my sins now carries my sorrows," said Flavia, almost triumphantly.

Sisidona had not recovered health and strength very rapidly, but she was progressing fairly now, and was able to go out in her litter occasionally; but she had not been to the temples, and Flaminius feared that this fact would soon be noticed and commented upon by her former friends, now that she was able to go out again.

Sisidona had foreseen this difficulty, and declined to go out as long as possible. But when the spring came her physician's orders were imperative; she must spend some hours of each day in the open air. "Not merely going to the temple and home again," added the physician, who did not know that his patient had given up the service to the gods. "Thou must leave the city behind thee, and get to the top of Mount Prion, or follow the course of our river Cayster for a few miles."

This prescription of her medical adviser Sisidona was inclined to quarrel with; but Flavia saw in it a relief from fashionable society, which she specially desired to avoid, both on her own and her sister's account now. Sisidona's long illness had been sufficient excuse for her non-attendance at banquets and festive gatherings of all kinds, for she could not attend these, she knew, without offending the prejudices of those who gave them,

IMPERATIVE: *a command*

by omitting the libations to the gods, or honouring the Lares and Penates at every meal; and for
her husband's sake she wished to avoid all possible
cause of offense.

Flavia likewise rejoiced, as it would give them
many opportunities for quiet converse they might
not otherwise have, for slaves were in such constant attendance upon them at home that it was
often no easy matter to be entirely free, and so she
readily seconded the physician's order.

"We will go in our litters as far as the Magne-
sian Gate, and then we will walk to a little hillock
in the valley beyond, where we can sit and rest,"
she said, eagerly; and Sisidona assented to the proposal when she saw how much her sister's heart
was set upon this plan.

So, early the next morning, they set off on their
trip, and before the city gate was reached Sisidona
began to feel stronger and better. It was a glorious morning. The sun was shining down upon the
fresh tender green of the budding myrtle hedges
that enclosed the sloping gardens, causing them to
glitter in his rays; while the gentle twitter of birds,
now busily engaged in building their nests in the
evergreen oaks and cork trees, and the murmur of
the rushing water of the Cayster on its way to the
sea, yielded pleasant music. All these sights and
sounds, from which Sisidona had so long been
shut out, awoke a feeling almost akin to gladness
in her heart, and she said, "I do not wonder that

men worship the gods of trees and fountains, and the earth itself, for it makes one feel glad to see these things in spite of others' sorrows."

"But to be able to worship their Creator, and to feel that He is not only thy God but thy Saviour and Friend as well, is not this better than all the beautiful allegories and fancies concerning the gods?" asked Flavia.

Sisidona's eyes were more eloquent than any words she could have spoken, and as she walked by her sister's side she pressed her hand in silent assent. "Flavia, wilt thou take me to thy Church? I should like to confess before man that I no longer believe in these dumb idols," said Sisidona, after a lengthened pause.

Flavia's face shone with the joy she felt at this avowal.

"God has heard and answered my prayers," she said; "and it will doubtless strengthen the faith of many to hear of thy conversion at this time."

After a walk of nearly an hour through a lovely region of orange groves and vineyards, skirting the foot of Mount Prion, where the breezes from the sea could gently fan the invalid's cheek, they reached a little quiet sequestered spot sacred to many hearts in Ephesus, and often visited by one and another who had never seen the sleeper beneath that lovely grass waving there, but had received new life from his words and treasured his command: "Little children, love one another;" for

SEQUESTERED: *secluded*

here rested the exile of Patmos, the beloved disciple, John; and sitting within sight of his tomb, Flavia told her sister all she had heard concerning his life, and of the hope many had cherished that he would tarry on earth until his Lord came the second time in glory.

"Oh, Flavia, if that glory could be revealed now!" exclaimed Sisidona, quickly. "If the Lord Christ should come in those clouds now slowly passing over the temple of Artemis, how confounded all her priests and priestesses would be! how astonished all Ephesus would be! Dost thou not long for that day to come?" she asked.

Flavia shook her head. "I do not think I do," she said, slowly and sadly. "I can—I do pray that God's kingdom may come in the hearts of men; and sometimes I think this kingdom of grace will come before the glory, impossible as it seems to us now."

"But, Flavia, dost thou not want the enemies of Christ confounded, the wicked swept off the earth?" exclaimed Sisidona.

"But who are the wicked?" inquired Flavia; "who are these enemies of Christ who are too proud to accept His salvation? My noble husband is one; our Emperor Marcus Aurelius is another; and—"

But Sisidona held up her hand. "I am selfish even in my effort to love Christ," she said. "I forget even Claudius in my wish to grasp the promised crown."

"The cross comes before the crown, little sister," said Flavia; "and we are often apt to forget that."

"But thou wilt help me to remember it, wilt thou not, Flavia, and thou wilt take me to the Christian Church the next time thou dost go, for I should like to become one of them as soon as I can, before thy great Sabbath if possible?"

"It shall be as thou dost desire, my sister, and we will eat our joyful paschal supper together this year. The Jews, from whom we take this feast, eat it with bitter herbs, in token of sorrow; but it can bring nothing but joy and blessed memories to a Christian, for it speaks to us of Him—'the Lamb of God which taketh away the sins of the world'[1]— and it will be indeed a joyful Easter to me when my sister sits down with me to commemorate the Lord's death."

The time passed all too quickly to the two ladies lingering there by the apostle's grave, talking of the glory that should be revealed when his feet again trod the streets of the beautiful city where many years of his life had been spent. Could anyone have told them that the very name of that city should pass away, and only a heap of ruins mark the spot where it stood; that the little hillock where they sat should in its name, "Ayasaluk," or "Holy Divine," alone tell where Ephesus the proud once flourished, they would have said it was impossible; and yet it is so at this day. A few half-wild shepherds live amid the ruins of Ephesus, but other inhabitants it has none. Her noble harbour is a salt

[1] JOHN 1:29

swamp, her shores deserted and utterly forgotten, for the Lord hath fulfilled His warning and removed her "candlestick out of his place," because she hid her light under a bushel in the day when it should have illumined all the nations round.

But at this time no such fate seemed possible, the streets were thronged with wealthy merchants or men skilled in the "curious arts" of Artemis; her market was full of bustling, energetic life, the sides of the circling hills clothed with gardens and vineyards, and her splendid harbour crowded with vessels from all parts of the world. Looking at the beautiful city as Flavia did, as she walked back to where she had left her slaves, the Lord's prediction seemed almost impossible of fulfillment; and yet their bishop was constantly repeating its warning words, and the ministers of the little congregations outside the walls were exhorted to teach their flocks to be true and faithful.

Flavia was one of the most regular and devout worshipers who used to meet in a large upper chamber of the bishop's house. Spies were often seen lurking round this neighbourhood, and the lady often feared that she should be recognized, perhaps arrested, for thus meeting with Christians, and she told her sister of this danger before they entered the city gates. But it did not alter Sisidona's determination. "I am not afraid," she said. "I have less to fear than thou hast." So a few weeks afterward Sisidona was admitted into Christ's visible Church, promising at her baptism to be His servant and soldier, to fight under His banner, and be loyal unto the end.

A few days later the sisters knelt together at the meeting for worship, which was followed the same evening by the Lord's Supper—the first and last time Sisidona partook of that holy ordinance in Ephesus. Flavia had been watched many times, and regular as Flaminius might be in his attendance at the temple of Artemis, everybody in the city knew that his wife was a Christian. They, however, feared to bring the charge against her at present. By-and-by, perhaps, it might be done more successfully, so they waited and watched still, and saw Sisidona come with her; and when this visit had been repeated a few times, they determined to accuse her of holding this superstition and forsaking the gods of Ephesus.

But before this charge could be formally brought forward, the proconsul, who had heard of it, and desired to escape such an unpleasant complication of affairs, advised Flaminius to withdraw from Ephesus for a time, and to try and induce his wife and her sister to give up all connection with this obstinate sect of Christians. The first part of this advice Flaminius readily agreed to act upon. To say that he was ill and needed a skillful physician was true enough; and so a journey to Pergamos was at once planned and prepared for, and people who knew the family secret wondered how it was that the wife of one so devoted to the gods could be a Christian.

CHAPTER XIV

PHILADELPHIA

WHILE the household of Flaminius were packing the linen and household goods—absolute necessaries for the long journey to Pergamos—their master went to the neighbouring city of Laodicea, to inquire whether disturbances had broken out there. It was not expected by the Roman governor that this city would give them much trouble in the question of their faith, for they were decorous, well-to-do people, by no means obstinate in the matter, and quite willing to sacrifice to the gods if trouble was likely to follow their refusal to do it. Indeed, it was done so complacently and with such a self-satisfied air, that those who saw it thought there could be little difference between the God of heaven, whom they professed to love and serve, and the gods of Olympus, whom their companions in other places called idols and demons.

Flaminius wished he had brought his wife with him when he heard this account. "They are sensible, worldly-wise people; I wish everybody was like them," he said.

DECOROUS: *proper, dignified*

"Things would be much more comfortable if others would take example by them, and be less hot about this superstition which they call Christianity," remarked the prefect, to whom Flaminius was speaking.

"Even so; but then, if this God of heaven, whom they profess to serve, is the only true God, as they say, I cannot quite understand how they can so easily worship the gods of Rome as you say they do."

"Nay, they can believe in any god they like, so that they are not too hot about it, and speak against the rest. It is a comfortable and pleasant way for everybody in Laodicea."

Comfortable and pleasant for the Roman governor. But what had been said by the Lord of this Laodicean Church about this very coolness which he had so commended? "I know thy works, that thou art neither cold nor hot: I would thou wert cold or hot. So then because thou art lukewarm, and neither cold nor hot, I will spue thee out of my mouth."[1]

Flaminius had never heard of this warning message—a warning not to Laodicea, but to Christians in all ages and all climes—and so he hastened back to assure the proconsul that no disturbance need be feared there, and to beg his wife to follow the example set by the Laodicean Christians.

But Flavia shook her head. "I dare not!" she said, "lest I share in their punishment, and be

[1] REVELATION 3:15-16

disowned by the Lord Jesus when He shall come again in glory."

To this Flaminius made no reply. Though he regretted, he could not but admire the calm steadfastness of his wife. The whole household were now busy making arrangements for the projected journey. It would be much longer than had been at first proposed. The duties of his office compelled Flaminius to make a detour so as to visit Philadelphia on his way northward to Pergamos. At length all was ready, and the ladies entered the litter which had been prepared for them, followed by Flaminius.

Most of the slaves had been left behind, but they still had a convoy of guards, bearers, slaves, and nurses in attendance on the children, numbering almost a hundred; so that, with these and the chariots and litters, the cavalcade was no inconsiderable one that slowly wound its way out of the gates of Ephesus, and took the mountain road toward the east. Once out of the city, Flavia could lift the silken hangings of her litter and watch the light, fleecy clouds passing over the deep azure sky, or note the aspect of the travelers they met on their way to the city, for the calends of May were beginning, and hundreds were eager to reach Ephesus to join in the festival of Artemis.

Looking on the gay, wealthy, eager throngs who were pressing forward now to join in the worship of the goddess, it seemed impossible that it

CALENDS OF MAY: *first day of May*

could ever be overthrown; that the despised Christians should ever be other than a downtrodden, oppressed people, poor and of no account either socially or politically, for society was on all hands ready to ban this new faith whenever it had the opportunity. That it progressed at all was in itself a standing miracle; but that it did daily gain fresh converts from the ranks of its enemies, in spite of all the persecutions organized against it, was a fact that no one could dispute, and was taken by its friends as a proof of its Divine origin. Flavia comforted herself and her sister with this thought, as they reclined upon their cushions, and watched the numerous travelers coming from all parts of Asia to be present at the great festival.

It was a weary, toilsome journey up the mountain road. They had now left the region of suburban villas with their trim gardens, and the date and olive plantations, and were soon wending their way through a forest of oaks and pines, where the breezes were chill and cold, and they had to keep a careful eye on each side of the path lest they should stumble on a wild boar, or no less savage robber, for these forests afforded shelter to many lawless bands who lived by plundering travelers. At length, after some hours' traveling, oaks and pines began to yield to poplars, vines, and myrtles, and the weary travelers knew that the most dangerous part of the forest was passed, and that

WENDING: *making*

they were nearing the plain on the western side of the mountain.

Flavia could now notice the little bubbling springs that trickled and filtered through the stones down the side of the hill; many of them joining after a little distance, and forming a brook of no mean use in that region, where no other refreshment could be obtained for man or beast.

A few miles farther on they came to a hostelry, where they found plentiful accommodation, the slaves sleeping in barns and outhouses, for Flaminius thought no more of his grooms and attendants than of his horses and mules, although he was considered a kind and considerate master by everybody.

The next part of their journey lay through a plain studded with olive-yards, citron and spice-groves, fields of cotton plants, wheat and barley, diversified with meadows where flowers dotted the fresh green grass, while every breeze came laden with the perfume of these and the blossoms of the orange-trees that grew so luxuriantly in all directions. To Flaminius, who had scarcely been beyond the city walls for a twelvemonth, and whose only relaxation from a wearisome round of duties had been a visit to the great amphitheater or the hippodrome, the sights and sounds everywhere greeting him were refreshing beyond description; and he ordered the cavalcade to travel slowly, and often came to a walk by the side of his wife's

MEAN: *unimportant*
HOSTELRY: *inn*
TWELVEMONTH: *year*

litter, or Flavia would alight, and they would walk together along the lonely country roads. There was but one drawback to their enjoyment of the lovely scene, and both felt it press heavily upon them at times. Flavia dared not give utterance to the glad thought that continually welled up in her heart, that these beauties by which they were surrounded were all the work of her Father in heaven, and proofs of His love to man, although they were so little regarded by him. Flaminius, too, would have liked to talk of the beauties of nature, but this would lead him to the stories of Rhea, and Ceres, and Flora, and Apollo, and a host of other deities whom Flavia called demons now, and so they often walked silently side by side, or talked of the children and the benefit they would derive from this journey.

At length they began to draw near the volcanic region in which Philadelphia was situated; then over the lava-strewn roads the cavalcade quickened their pace, and the gates of the city were reached before they had any idea they were so close. The usual landmarks by which travelers were guided were almost entirely wanting, for every tower and lofty building had been overthrown, and Philadelphia was only half-inhabited and wholly in ruins. Very different did its deserted streets look from the crowded thoroughfares of Ephesus; and its inhabitants were not gay, fashionable people, who tried to outdo each other in the splendid appointments of their gilded chariots or the richness of their jeweled harness and splendour of their robes, but quiet, hard-working people, who had no choice but to stay in their half-ruined city. Steady, thoughtful, resolute men they looked; and Flavia, recalling the commendation this Church had received for patience and holding fast that which they had received from their teacher, Quadratus, one of John's own pupils, wondered how the Gospel prospered now in this time of persecution.

The coming of so distinguished a visitor as the Roman patrician caused quite a sensation in the half-depopulated town; but the Christians feared his visit boded no good to them. Their astonishment may therefore be imagined when Flavia and her sister sought out their minister soon after they arrived, and presented a letter of greeting and kind inquiry after their state from their brethren at Ephesus.

While Flavia by this visit was cheering the hearts and strengthening the faith of this little band of true-hearted witnesses, her husband was receiving from the prefect a doleful account of their obstinacy and uncompromising refusal to worship any of the national gods.

Flaminius looked disconcerted when he heard this, for he had hoped that these people were like the Laodiceans, and that a little friendly intercourse with them would convince Flavia that she was needlessly obstinate in holding so fast

DOLEFUL: *gloomy*
DISCONCERTED: *unsettled*
INTERCOURSE: *conversation*

to this God of hers, to the utter rejection of all others. He had felt so confident that things were as he wished in this respect, that he had readily agreed to her seeking Quadratus, hoping by this means to induce her to yield to his wishes, in which case they might return to Ephesus instead of taking the long journey to Pergamos. His health would soon improve if the cause of his anxiety were thus removed, and there would be no need to convince people that he did not share in his wife's superstition by going to the far-famed god of health, for she herself would refute the charge brought against her by going sometimes to the temple of Diana as well as to the secret gatherings of the Christians, which he would not ask her to give up.

The prefect saw that his visitor was depressed and troubled; but Flaminius was by no means disposed to trust him with the dangerous secret that often cost him anxious days and sleepless nights, and resolved to leave Philadelphia before it could be known to anyone. The business he had come upon, which was to impress the prefect with the necessity of pleasing the Jews just now, at all costs, since they were wealthy and powerful in the State, was soon accomplished, and with little more than a passing glance at the prostrate columns, statues, and arches that lay in shattered heaps all round, he took his way along the great Roman road toward the north.

"How is it, my Flaminius, that this city is left a

heap of ruins?" asked Flavia, as they once more began their march onward.

"The empire is not so wealthy as it once was; and though the Government helped to restore Ephesus and Smyrna, Thyatira and Sardis, it was not deemed wise to rebuild Philadelphia, situated as it is in a region where earthquakes are so frequent," said Flaminius, glancing back at the shattered marble columns and gateways that testified so eloquently of the violence of the shock it had suffered.

"Poor Philadelphia—rich Philadelphia!" exclaimed Flavia, as the sun lighted up its white stone walls.

"Rich Philadelphia!" repeated her husband. "The place is the poorest in the province of Lystra."

Flavia coloured, and a painful sense that what she deemed true riches her husband would count the greatest poverty, came over her. "It would be considered poor, I doubt not; and yet it seems a pity that its name should die."

"But it must die—the place is doomed," said Flaminius, rather testily. "If they wanted the name of the prince after whom it was named to live through ages, they should have given some other city this name, for now Philadelphia will speedily be forgotten by the world."

"Nay, it was not so much the prince I was thinking of," said Flavia, absently.

TESTILY: *irritably*

"Brotherly love," said Flaminius; "that is one of the things these obstinate Christians believe in, the prefect told me."

Flavia raised her eyes to her husband's face. "Are the Christians of Philadelphia to be persecuted?" she asked timidly.

"Persecuted!" repeated Flaminius. "That is rather a hard word, Flavia. We must yield to the wish of the people in these cities, which are only half-Romanized, and if they demand that these Christians should be compelled to give up their strange worship we are compelled to accede to the demand."

"And these Christians of Philadelphia?" said Flavia, questioningly.

"That will depend upon their old enemies, the Jews. Just now, when the emperor must impose heavy taxes to meet the expenses of the war, these Jews must be pleased at all costs, for they are the chief merchants and traffickers in these provinces."

"But the Jews are allowed to meet in their synagogues without hindrance," said Flavia; "and they worship the same God that we do."

Flaminius smiled. "I know nothing of thy God," he said; "but I know the Jews and Christians hate each other, and that it is the Jews who are so frequently complaining of them."

Flavia attempted to explain the difference that existed between the two, but Flaminius hastily

ACCEDE: *give consent, agree*

interrupted her. "I cannot listen to this," he said; "thy God is nothing to me, and I am nothing to Him;" saying which he escorted her back to her litter and mounted his chariot once more.

Flavia looked sad as she lay back on her cushions beside her sister, and Sisidona noticed it.

"Is not Flaminius so well?" she asked.

"It was not of my husband alone I was thinking, but our brethren of Philadelphia, who I fear will soon be given up to the fury of their enemies again," said Flavia, with a deep sigh.

"Did Flaminius tell thee this?" asked Sisidona.

"Yes; the Jews must be pleased at all costs just now;" and Flavia drew from her broad embroidered girdle a small roll of parchment. "These are the messages sent by the mouth of John from the Lord Himself to the Churches of Lydia and Mysia, and our brethren of Philadelphia will need the comfort of theirs, I doubt not. Listen, Sisidona. 'Because thou hast kept the word of My patience, I also will keep thee from the hour of temptation, which shall surely come upon all the world, to try them that dwell upon the earth.'[1] Yes, the Lord will stand by them, though the Romans may give them up to the fury of the Jews," she said, as she replaced her precious manuscript, and thought how often she had tested the truth of the promises she had read during the last twelvemonth.

[1] REVELATION 3:10

CHAPTER XV

AT PERGAMOS

SEVERAL weeks were spent in traveling from Philadelphia to Pergamos, for more than once they had to make a prolonged stay at some of the villages at which they halted, for Flaminius was taken seriously ill when they were a few miles from the former city; but he persistently refused to have a physician called to him. The god of healing, Esculapius, would restore him to perfect health as soon as he could reach his temple, he said; and all Flavia's persuasions to allow her to send for assistance before they came to their journey's end were useless. Once or twice Flavia feared he would be unable to accomplish the journey. Painful as it was to know that her husband sought for restored health through the divination of an idol priest, she could not but feel thankful when the lofty conical hill that gave its name to Pergamos was in view. They pressed on toward the fortified mountain or "burg" with renewed energy, and a few hours saw them in the beautiful valley that was

CONICAL: *cone-shaped*

crowded with temples to Apollo and Jupiter, Diana and Venus, as well as to the favourite deity Esculapius, with his familiar companion, a huge serpent, which was said to have taught him the art of healing.

Unlike Ephesus or Philadelphia, Pergamos was beautiful by nature rather than by art. Groves of the choicest and loveliest trees skirted the fortified mountains, and beneath the shadow of these were statues and altars of every deity of Greece and Rome. To these came invalids with their friends, an almost endless crowd of worshipers, each, like Flaminius, confident that the son of Apollo could restore them to health. Accompanied by two of his chief slaves, Flaminius went to sacrifice to Esculapius the very day of his arrival, and having performed all the rites prescribed by the flamen, he decided to sleep in the sacred temple, as he heard that the remedy for his disease could only be communicated in the sacred shadow of its walls and during the hours of darkness.

Flavia was not aware of this when he left her, and so one of the slaves was dispatched to inform her that Flaminius would sleep in the temple to meet the saviour-god, as he was called, and would return early the next day. She was sitting with her sister and her children when the message was delivered, and she could not repress a shiver of horror as she heard the name Esculapius had assumed to himself.

"The saviour-god!" she repeated. "Sisidona, we will pray tonight that the true Saviour may be revealed to my noble Flaminius;" and so, while he lay sleeping within the sacred shadow of Esculapius and his serpent, Flavia wrestled with God in prayer on behalf of her blinded but beloved husband.

Unlike most of his compeers at this time, who believed in nothing in heaven or earth, and conformed to the usages of society in worshiping the gods merely because it was fashionable, and a means of keeping down the poor and ignorant multitude, Flaminius was a true and devout disciple of the Olympian deities; and so when he awoke the next morning from a sound sleep, it was with a feeling of disappointment he discovered that he was no better than when he entered the temple. Suddenly, however, he remembered that the remedy was to be revealed to him by the god, and he tried to recollect whether he had seen a vision or been visited by Esculapius, in any form: but he could recall nothing. His sleep had been entirely dreamless, so far as he could remember, and he was about to leave the temple, feeling both vexed and mystified, when a flamen appeared and kindly inquired after the state of his health.

Flaminius told him he felt no better for sleeping in the temple, and expressed his disappointment that no remedy had been revealed to him either. A smile of mingled scorn and pity curled the flamen's lip for a moment.

COMPEERS: *equals in rank*

"I am not surprised," he said; "it often happens thus; but be not disquieted. We have a college of medicine adjoining this temple, and I am one of its physicians."

Flaminius looked at the man in his long white robes. "A physician, and not a flamen?" he said, slowly.

"Yes, I am both, and I find full occupation," he said.

"But I came not to this shrine of healing to consult a physician, but to be cured by the god himself," said Flaminius.

"And art thou so besotted and blind that thou dost believe with the ignorant multitude all—"

"I believe that Esculapius can heal me," interrupted Flaminius, angrily.

"Then let him do it!" retorted the flamen; and turning on his heel he walked away.

Flaminius gazed after him for a moment, a tide of bitter, resentful feeling taking possession of his heart. So these physicians robbed the god of his honour by pretending to cure patients with their vile decoctions. Little wonder was it that the Christians spoke against the gods, when even their own servants acted so dishonourably; and he went home highly incensed with the flamen.

Flavia met him with a look of anxious concern upon her countenance, but Flaminius would not impart to her the secret cause of his annoyance.

BESOTTED: *drunken*
DECOCTIONS: *extracts obtained by boiling down*
INCENSED: *infuriated*

"I slept too soundly last night, Flavia," he said, in answer to her questioning look. "I will offer another sacrifice today, and ask the priest to make a special inquiry on my behalf:" and having rested and taken a bath, two white doves were procured, and with these, and a good sum in Roman gold, Flaminius once more sought the far-famed shrine of Esculapius.

Borne in a litter, with such a train of slaves in attendance as became his rank, Flaminius once more entered the sacred grove, and alighting at the steps he hastened to present his offering and sacrifice to the officiating flamen. A crowd of priests in long white robes, each bearing a wand, around which a serpent was entwined, lined the approach to the altar; and to one of these Flaminius made known his desire to consult the oracle of the god without delay.

"We will carefully inspect the entrails and make known the result," said the priest, in a hollow whisper. The sacrificing priest received the birds from his attendant, and one was fastened down by the cord to two rings fixed at the side of the altar so that it lay on its back, and though it struggled, could not move from the spot. With one stroke the breast was opened, and the priest, with his keen-bladed knife, took out the liver and entrails almost as soon as its death-struggle had ceased, and then, while it was being consumed amid the odours of myrrh and frankincense, he proceeded to examine them very carefully. The brain of the second bird was examined instead of the liver, and both being declared to augur a favourable reply from the god, a low chant was taken up by the whole band, which grew quicker as they proceeded, until at last it amounted to almost a scream, when one, rushing forward toward the figure of the god himself, shrieked and danced and leaped like one possessed.

At length came a low hollow sound, the chant sank to a low cadence, and the chief priest ceased his exertions, and fell prostrate to the ground in the attitude of reverential listening to the voice of the god. He interpreted the words that were spoken, for no one but he could understand that voice, and these were communicated to an augur standing near, and by him borne to the anxious Flaminius.

"Sleep in the temple tonight," was the message he again received; and feeling anything but pleased at the result of his errand, he went home, resolving, however, to obey the command once more. That he might not be so drowsy again he rested during the remaining hours of the day, and, after acquainting Flavia with his intention of passing another night in the temple, he ordered his litter, and reached the sacred edifice soon after sunset.

There was little fear of his sleeping tonight. He was not only anxious to be cured of the disease that he knew was slowly but surely sapping the

AUGUR: *foretell*
CADENCE: *rhythm*

springs of his life, but he felt jealous of the honour of Esculapius, and was anxious to defend him from the sneers of these physicians who sought to rob him of his due honour by declaring that he could not heal his votaries without their assistance, for such he found was the general belief in Pergamos.

So, instead of lying down on the mattress provided, as on the previous night, he sat near the entrance and watched the hosts of glittering stars as they came out one by one, shining down from the deep purple heavens like burning eyes that would scorch and consume all that offended them in this lower sphere. That, at least, was the fancy that took possession of the mind of Flaminius tonight, for in the shadowy stillness of the temple he had time to conjure up all kinds of imaginings; but this was the one that took the greatest hold of him, and remained with him most persistently. From the reverie into which this had plunged him he was aroused by the sound of voices singing a low chant, not unlike a funeral dirge; and moving a little nearer to the open space and listening intently, he could recognize distinctly the dialect of Greek spoken in the district. He could understand the words, too, but they startled him not a little, for, although a funeral dirge, it spoke of the land of shades as a land of light and peace and joy. Could it be possible that any mourner could entertain such wild hopes as these? Surely it must

REVERIE: *being lost in thought*
DIRGE: *mournful song*

be a band of lunatics, for who ever heard of such anticipations as these being cherished?

But he had heard of this strange belief before, and he suddenly remembered that his wife had once attempted to explain it to him; but he had stopped her, as, being connected with the forbidden subject of her religion, he could not listen to it. Now, however, that he had nothing to do but watch the stars and wait the coming of Esculapius, he thought he might beguile the time by listening for a few minutes to this Christian hymn; it would do him no harm, and Flavia need not know of it; and so he placed himself near one of the pillars, just where he could hear most advantageously.

He almost shuddered as he listened, for the hymn that was sung seemed to breathe aloud the reverie he had been indulging, for it spoke of God looking down from His dwelling-place in heaven upon all the sons of men—looking with tenderest pity and love upon all, but especially upon those who had accepted His offer of peace and salvation through Jesus Christ.

"Jesus Christ!" repeated Flaminius; "then there are Christians here, and this is a Christian funeral;" and he left the sacred enclosure, and keeping under the shadow of the trees silently drew near the spot from whence the singing proceeded. The body had been lowered into the grave, and the singing was concluded; but the service was not yet over, it seemed, for an elderly man was speaking

BEGUILE: *pass*

to the little crowd of mourners and friends gathered round, bidding them not sorrow as those without hope, for their Lord and Master, who had passed into the heavens beyond their sight, had called the departed one into His immediate presence, where, with saints and angels, she was now singing the praise of Him who had washed her in His own blood, and made her faultless by His own grace, having redeemed her from the evil of the world and of her own sinful nature.

Under the shadow of an almond-tree the Roman nobleman heard words he had never heard before. Could they be true, or were these people really deceived? Certainly they were in earnest, for there was no aim at effect—no seeking to attract the attention or to impress its votaries with any mystery or awe at this midnight funeral; and as Flaminius crept back to the temple he felt glad that he was in the proconsulate of Mysia, instead of being within the bounds of his own jurisdiction, for it would be no breach of duty for him to keep what he had heard a secret now, as it might be if they were near Ephesus.

All through the hours of the night he pondered over what he had heard, and almost started when the first streak of dawn came slowly stealing over the marble pavement at his feet. No voice had as yet broken the stillness of the silent temple, and Flaminius, as a relief to his troubled thoughts, slowly passed out to the open space once more, and turning his face toward the east watched the stars fade out one by one before the golden radiance that came streaming over all the sky just before the god of day himself appeared.

Flaminius stood and gazed at the charming vision of beauty as it gradually unfolded one glory after another, bathing everything in its golden glow; and there arose in his mind one of the questions of the night. Was there, after all, but one God who created the heavens and the earth? and was Apollo a mere fiction of man's brain? The boldness of such a thought shocked Flaminius, and he returned to the temple to watch and wait a little longer.

Certainly his faith in Esculapius was very much shaken, and he questioned his right to the term of saviour now. Shortly afterward a flamen appeared, and repeated the question of the previous morning.

"I have neither seen nor heard anything!" answered Flaminius.

"Then thou must put thyself under the care of the physicians. We are too wise not to have a college of medicine near the temple," answered the flamen, complacently.

"Art thou in earnest?" asked Flaminius.

"Quite so," replied the man. "Thou art not one of the ignorant multitude, and so thou dost not need to be told that it is necessary to keep up the rites and ceremonies of the temple to keep them in subjection, for thou knowest it, and so I will be confidential, and tell thee Esculapius is no better than the rest. His shrine has worshipers, because the physicians heal the sick in his name; but they could do just as well without it; but the ignorant must be impressed. Besides, there are priests, augurs, and slaves, almost without number, to be supported out of the offerings made to him."

Flaminius listened in a sort of stupid wonder to what the man said. He had heard the same concerning other gods again and again, but it never entered beyond his brain. Now, however, a veil seemed suddenly to be torn away, and a conviction that the man was speaking the truth at last pierced through brain and heart alike. Silently he passed out of the temple a few minutes afterwards—passed out with every belief in the power of the gods overthrown and in ruins.

STUPID: *stunned*

CHAPTER XVI

SATAN'S SEAT

FLAVIA was greatly disappointed when she heard that Flaminius had decided to pass a second night in the temple of Esculapius, and this feeling was intensified when her sister related what she had heard from some of the members of the Church here concerning the god worshiped at Pergamos.

Flavia had been charged with a letter of greeting from the Bishop of Ephesus to his co-worker in the Gospel at Pergamos, and, being unable to deliver this herself at once, Sisidona had taken it. But on reaching the house of the bishop she heard that his wife was dead, and was to be buried that evening, and at the same time a cordial invitation was given her to attend the funeral; while, in a conversation she had with the bishop's daughter, she was told to be careful not to talk about this before strangers, as a great deal of active enmity had been shown lately by the priests of the Evil One towards the Christians.

ENMITY: *hostility*

"The priests of the Evil One," repeated Flavia, when her sister related the conversation to her.

"Yes," answered Sisidona. "Pergamos is really where Satan's seat is, and where Satan dwelleth; for this worship of Esculapius is only the slightest modification of the worship of the Evil One, represented by his companion, the serpent."

"And my noble Flaminius will bow down to that old serpent the devil, and refuse to worship the God of heaven, the Father of light! Oh, Sisidona, what shall I do?"

"We can only pray for him, my sister."

"But I have prayed—prayed and waited and hoped," said Flavia, rising from her seat and pacing up and down the chamber in her agitation.

"Flavia, do not despair," whispered Sisidona, gently. "The Lord can use the most unlikely means for the accomplishment of His purpose."

But Flavia shook her head. "Flaminius seems more wholly given to the worship of this god than ever before," she said; "and to think it is Satan himself thus ignorantly worshiped is worse than all."

To turn the conversation, Sisidona spoke of the funeral that was to take place, and asked if her sister would accompany her, but Flavia declined.

"Neither of the children is quite well," she said; "and I should prefer being alone this evening while Flaminius is at the temple."

"Not alone, Flavia," whispered her sister, gently;

"for thou knowest the promises, 'Lo, I am with you alway, even unto the end of the world,'[1] and 'Whatsoever ye shall ask the Father in My name, He will do it.'"[2]

"I have been forgetful of the promises, and faithless of late, I fear," said Flavia, with a deep-drawn sigh, as she returned her sister's embrace, for Sisidona had arranged to attend a short service at the church before going to the funeral.

It was not surprising that Flavia should feel depressed at this time, for the critical condition of her husband's health, and the prolonged journey they had just accomplished, made her both anxious and weary, and one's mental and spiritual condition is more dependent upon the physical health and strength than many suppose.

After Sisidona had gone out and the children had been visited, Flavia returned to her chamber, and dismissing her attendant slaves, prepared to pass the night in prayer and reading from the parchment-roll the promises of God, which were all "yea and amen" to her "in Christ Jesus."[3] Was it strange that as she read and wrestled with God in prayer in behalf of her beloved husband light and joy should suddenly fill her soul, chasing all the darkness of doubt from her mind, and giving her the blessed assurance that her prayers would yet be answered?

It was late when Sisidona returned, so she did not go to her sister's chamber to deliver the

---

[1] MATTHEW 28:20   [2] JOHN 16:23
[3] II CORINTHIANS 1:20

message sent by the bishop, who, in spite of his own grief and sorrow at this time, was not unmindful of the strangers who had come to sojourn with them for a season, and who had thought it needful to send a word of warning against offending the prejudices of the priests or worshipers of Esculapius. Sisidona herself had been somewhat puzzled by several things she had seen and heard among her fellow-Christians, for while some maintained that the worship of this son of Apollo was tantamount to honouring the prince of evil himself, others declared that an idol, being simply an image of wood or stone, outward compliance with forms and ceremonies was of no moment either way, and so, to save giving offense, they joined in many practices which some of the brethren thought to be idolatrous.

Sisidona was telling her sister of this as they sat together in the garden the next morning, when one of the slaves came to announce that his master had returned, for Flavia had given orders to the porter to send to the garden when Flaminius came home.

"We will talk of this matter further, my Sisidona," she said, as she rose from her seat and followed the slave to her husband's room.

Almost trembling with doubt and fear, lest by the arts of divination Flaminius had been induced to give himself up, body and soul, to this satanic god, Flavia timidly inquired after his health, and

TANTAMOUNT TO: *the equivalent of*
MOMENT: *importance*

whether he had slept during the night.

Flaminius started at the question, and looked keenly at his wife. "Wert thou at that funeral last night?" he asked, hastily.

Flavia shook her head, for she in turn was so surprised at his question that she could not reply audibly.

"But thou knowest there was a funeral last night?" said Flaminius, noticing her confusion.

"Yes; the wife of the minister of the Church here was buried," answered Flavia.

"I knew it was a Christian funeral," said Flaminius; and then he turned to gaze out of the little casement near which he was sitting.

Flavia came to his side and fell upon her knees. "My husband, thou hast not come to rouse up the spirit of persecution here!" she almost gasped.

Flaminius looked down into her white, terror-stricken face. "I could not persecute these people now," he said, in a whisper; and then a spasm of mental agony crossed his face, and it grew white and rigid in the intensity of his emotion.

His wife was greatly alarmed. "Thou art ill, my Flaminius," she said; and she was about to summon the slave from the anteroom; but he laid his hand upon her shoulder detainingly.

"No, no," he said; "I am no worse, and that false god could do me no good."

"And thou art greatly disappointed, my Flaminius," said Flavia.

ANTEROOM: *outer room*

"It is not that alone, but I have no god now. The hosts of Olympus have failed me, for I have at last discovered that their power is all a delusion and a lie."

Flavia clasped her hands, and could scarcely repress an exclamation of joy as she heard this. "My prayers have been answered!" she said, half-aloud, but her husband did not notice the exclamation. He was gazing out of the window, again lost in his own painful thoughts.

"I am the poorest wretch on the face of the earth!" he exclaimed, in a minute or two, "for I have no god."

"Nay, nay, my Flaminius, but the one true God is about to reveal Himself to thee. He hath shown thee the vanity of this idol-worship that He may win thee to His service," said Flavia, quickly.

"It is too late for that," answered Flaminius. "I have grown to manhood in the service of Jupiter and Juno, and I cannot change my religion as we change the fashion of our clothes."

"Nay, but when we have seen the folly of our ways it behooveth us to learn wherein we have been foolish, and set ourselves diligently in the path of wisdom," answered Flavia.

"But where is the path of wisdom?" asked Flaminius. "We have no light, no guidance by which to find it, even if there be such a path."

"My husband, there is such a light to guide the wandering footsteps of man to the fount of wisdom, even God Himself; the God of heaven and earth, who has promised His Spirit to be our unerring Guide," said Flavia, earnestly.

"What is it thou speakest of—what is this light thou talkest about?" asked Flaminius.

"The message of God to man—the Word of God contained in the Scriptures," said Flavia.

"And hast thou this message?" asked her husband, with some curiosity.

"I have the whole record of the life of Jesus Christ, the Son of God, who came to make known the will of God the Father, and afterward died for the sins and iniquities of the world. He is the true, the only Saviour-God, and believing in Him we have eternal life."

"Go on, and tell me something more concerning this strange doctrine," said Flaminius, as Flavia paused.

She needed no second bidding, both forgetting the lapse of time and that Flaminius needed food and rest after his protracted vigil, until one of the slaves announced that the meal had been spread some time, and that Sisidona was awaiting them. Then Flaminius suddenly became aware of a weakness and faintness that was almost overpowering, and Flavia noticed that her husband looked very ill.

"I have been thoughtless and unwise, my Flaminius," she said, as she directed the slave to fetch some restoratives, and request Sisidona to come to her.

PROTRACTED: *long, drawn out*

It was evident that the excitement of the last few hours had overtaxed the invalid's strength, and a doctor had to be summoned almost immediately, for he grew so rapidly worse that Flavia was seriously alarmed for his recovery.

The doctor's first order was that he should be at once taken to the temple and various rites performed there on his behalf. This, however, Flavia positively refused to comply with.

"My husband has already spent two nights in the temple of Esculapius," she said, with emotion, "and is worse rather than better."

"And he received no direction as to a remedy?" asked the doctor, in a tone of well-feigned surprise.

Flavia fixed her clear, truthful eyes full upon him. "Thou knowest that this pretended god is a false saviour," she said, sternly.

The physician looked abashed. "I knew not that thou hadst thrown off the trammels of a superstition so necessary for science and art and all good government," he said, by way of excuse; and then he proceeded to examine his patient more carefully, and make various inquiries necessary to a right understanding of his complaint.

After some little time spent in this way he ordered some preparations made from herbs growing in the neighbourhood, but there was no mention of charms or divinations or sacrifices to be offered to Esculapius, and he assured Flavia that

WELL-FEIGNED: *well-pretended*
ABASHED: *ashamed*
TRAMMELS: *restraints*

what her husband needed more than anything else was rest of body and mind.

"He must not return to his duties at Ephesus for a year at least, and he had better live in retirement, avoiding all excitement and over-exertion," said the physician, as he rose to take his departure.

Flavia thanked him, and promised a ready compliance with this part of his advice, for it accorded entirely with her own wishes upon the subject, and she had not the least doubt but that Flaminius would concur with it likewise. Who can picture the joy she felt as she recalled their conversation? The thought that her beloved husband was anxious to know more concerning the truth and authority of God's Word, lifted her above the present trouble and distress entirely. She almost failed to realize his present dangerous condition, and felt neither weariness, fatigue, nor anxiety, while watching by his bedside tenderly ministering to his wants, or answering some of his many doubts and questionings with a passage of God's Word.

At length Flaminius, like Sisidona, was able to grasp the sublime yet simple truth that "God was in Christ, reconciling the world unto Himself, not imputing their trespasses unto them...For He hath made Him to be sin for us, who knew no sin; that we might be made the righteousness of God in Him."[1]

Flaminius was as decided, too, in his abhorrence of all idol-worship, and before he could leave his

---

[1] II CORINTHIANS 5:19,21

SUBLIME: *exalted*

ABHORRENCE: *hatred*

chamber gave orders that the images of his ancestors, the Lares and Penates so carefully treasured
and brought with them from Rome, should be removed from their place of honour near the *impluvium* in the center of the *atrium*, and packed away
in the chests in which they had been brought.

The statues of Jupiter and Diana were likewise
removed from their pedestals and placed out of
sight, greatly to the horror of some of the slaves,
who feared that this act of impiety would be fear-
fully avenged by the mighty Thunderer, whose
power they had been taught to fear.

But day after day passed, and no calamity be-
fell either Flaminius or his household. He gained
strength rapidly, and was soon able to take daily
exercise in the garden, and receive the visits of the
Church members. Flavia had informed them of

IMPLUVIUM: *reservoir for collecting rainwater*

the change in her husband, and of his desire to become a member of Christ's visible Church, so that some of these visits were official as well as friendly. Flaminius had been accepted as a catechumen or candidate, and his baptism would take place as soon as he could go to the Church. The Christians of Pergamos thought Flaminius had been unwise and imprudent in banishing all the private and national gods from his household, and feared it would draw upon them the notice of their neighbours, and might be the cause of much trouble.

Flavia, however, upheld her husband, maintaining that honouring an idol was dishonouring to the God of heaven, and she afterwards read to him the warning addressed to this Church, from the roll of parchment she possessed, recording the messages to the seven Churches of Asia: "I know thy works, and where thou dwellest, even where Satan's seat is: and thou holdest fast My name, and hast not denied My faith, even in those days wherein Antipas was My faithful martyr, who was slain among you, where Satan dwelleth. But I have a few things against thee, because thou hast there them that hold the doctrine of Balaam, who taught Balac to cast a stumbling-block before the children of Israel, to eat things sacrificed unto idols, and to commit fornication. So hast thou also them that hold the doctrine of the Nicolaitanes, which thing I hate. Repent; or else I will come unto thee quickly, and will fight against them with the sword of My mouth."[1]

---

[1] REVELATION 2:13-16
IMPRUDENT: *rash*

"Who are these Nicolaitanes?" asked Flaminius.

"They are a sect of the Gnostics, or knowers, and they would make the religion of Christ accommodate itself either to philosophy or idolatry," answered Flavia.

"And these Gnostics, or knowers, are they Christians?" asked Flaminius. "I never heard of them before."

"I know not what to call them but the enemies of Christ," replied Flavia. "They do not believe that the world was made by God, the Father of lights, but by an inferior being. They do not believe in Christ being the Son of God, equal to the Father, or that He really took man's nature upon Him, as the Scriptures declare. They likewise deny that Christ died to redeem the world: so that, to believe in their doctrine, we must disbelieve the record of the Scriptures entirely."

"And these people have crept into the Church of Pergamos?" asked Flaminius.

"They have crept into many churches, and their principles are partly, if not wholly, adopted by many more. I greatly fear that here in Pergamos they have great power, in spite of the warning message sent by the Lord Himself," added Flavia, with a sigh.

"Then we will not linger here longer than is needful," said Flaminius, decidedly. "As soon as I am strong enough to travel, we will fix our abode in some other city, until we return to Ephesus."

CHAPTER XVII

AT THYATIRA

FLAMINIUS was for some time undecided whether he would return at once to Rome or remove a little farther northward to the town of Adramyttium, but a slight circumstance at length induced him to remove to Thyatira, which was on the road to Ephesus.

The first view the party had of this old Macedonian city was by no means prepossessing; for though her people might not disdain art in any of its varied forms, they were too busy to give much attention to it, for the manufacture of many articles of use in daily life occupied all their time. Potters and tanners, weavers and dyers, seldom leave a name in the world; but the world could get on better without its sculptors and painters than without these more humble workers. And so Asia might be very proud of her beautiful Ephesus, with its matchless temple of Diana, but she could not have got on without Thyatira, with its dirty narrow streets, its smoke-grimed houses, and noisy

PREPOSSESSING: *favorable*

din of looms and potteries, where cloth was woven and pots and pans prepared for use.

The purple robes of the emperor and his senators often came from the looms of Thyatira, and it was a trader in these purple robes traveling in the way of business who first heard Paul preach at Philippi and brought the glorious news of salvation home to her native city. Thyatira had not had the privileges of Ephesus; but whereas the Lord had complained of the favoured Ephesian Church that she had "left her first love" and her "first works," Thyatira is commended for her works, and charity, and patience, for the Saviour had declared "the last to be more than the first,"[1] so that her business cares were not allowed to choke the seed of God's Word first sown by the purple-seller, Lydia, but they had learned the blessed secret of making the best of both worlds, remembering the apostle's exhortation, "Not slothful in business, fervent in spirit, serving the Lord."[2]

But Thyatira was not wholly Christian—far from it. There were splendid temples to Jupiter and Venus, and Agenoria, the goddess of industry; and the Christian citizens were only there on sufferance. But still, while doing their work in the world they did not forget that they were citizens of the New Jerusalem, and so proved themselves faithful servants to the charge committed to them, that men, seeing their good works, glorified their Father in heaven by following in their footsteps, so

[1] MATTHEW 19:30   [2] ROMANS 12:11

THERE ON SUFFERANCE: *tolerated*

that the Church grew not only in faith and love,
but in numbers and influence likewise.

When Flaminius and his family reached their
destination, however, this Church was in some
consternation, owing to the arrest of several of
its members. They had lived so many years now
in uninterrupted peace that they forgot the fact
that old laws might at any time be revived against
them, and so this fresh persecution plunged them
into the deepest distress.

The coming of a Roman official, who was himself a Christian, seemed to the perplexed Church
a direct interposition of God in their behalf, for
no lawyer in Thyatira would undertake to plead
for a sect now so unpopular as these Christians.

So, almost before the strangers were settled in
their new abode, the bishop came to pay them a
visit, and to request Flaminius to undertake the
cause of his oppressed flock when the prisoners
were summoned to appear before the prefect.
Flavia warmly seconded the bishop's request, and
was both surprised and disappointed that her husband hesitated to accede to it at once. He was a
Christian, and openly avowed it at Pergamos; was
he going to become timid at the first breath of
persecution, and deny his profession at Thyatira?
she asked, when the bishop left without having obtained the favour he came to request.

Flaminius looked hurt for a moment, but soon
recovered himself, and with a smile said, "My

CONSTERNATION: *sudden alarm and dismay*
INTERPOSITION: *intervention*

impulsive Flavia, I cannot act hastily in this matter. For thy sake and our children's I must count the cost of such a proceeding as this," he added.

Flavia looked at him in some surprise. "Flaminius, couldst thou not plead for the Christians now as thou formerly pleaded against them?" she asked.

"I *could* do so, doubtless; but, my Flavia, I am not, as thou knowest, a wealthy man, and sesterces do not fall from the skies," said Flaminius.

Flavia began to comprehend now the difficult position in which her husband was placed, but she hastened to assure him that if he could not return to Ephesus to resume his duties there, the Lord would provide for him elsewhere.

"But it is not that alone that troubles me at this time," answered Flaminius. "As the representative of Marcus Aurelius, it is my duty to plead against these people, who are accused of disturbing the peace of the empire; and for the performance of these duties I have already received a considerable sum to enable me to go to Pergamos without difficulty. Now, what will it be, if I, a servant of the emperor, assist those whom he deems his enemies?"

"Oh, Flaminius, then thou canst not help these persecuted Christians?" inquired Flavia, bursting into tears.

"I know not; I cannot tell; I must think of what can be done," answered Flaminius. "Hush, my Flavia, we must seek the guidance of God's Spirit in this difficulty; it may be He will direct us by a way we know not—a way by which I may serve my brethren in Christ without being treacherous towards the emperor."

This was the only consolation available in the present difficulty; but Flavia, though she neglected not to make it a matter of prayer, had very little hope of a favourable solution of the difficulty. To her surprise, however, Flaminius came to her the next morning with a far less anxious face than he had worn of late, for, in spite of his improving health and the happiness they now enjoyed in Christian communion with each other, a cloud of anxious foreboding had again begun to settle down upon Flaminius, which his wife failed to penetrate.

Now, however, it seemed to be dispelled, for the time at least, and Flaminius said, "I think I can see a way out of the difficulty, my Flavia, if thou wilt help me."

"I help thee, Flaminius? Is it possible I can help thee?" she said, with a joyful smile.

"Yes, indeed, for without thee I am powerless in this strait; and, my Flavia, if thou hadst not already proved thyself a woman more worthy than most of our Roman dames I could not venture to take this step. My Flavia, thou didst prefer to direct the ways of thy household when thou becamest a Christian, and doing this, and thy having little love of display, have enabled me to lay aside some portion

STRAIT: *difficulty*

of my income; and I have thought that we could live in retirement with a small household of slaves, and the sale of the rest would enable me to refund all I have received since the calends of May."

Flavia clasped her hands in joyful surprise. "My Flaminius, wilt thou be able to plead for our brethren here in Thyatira?" she asked.

"Not only for these, I trust, but for all who are desolate and persecuted; for I have thought I might honour my Lord and do some service to His saints if I devoted myself to this work; and I thank God and thee, my Flavia, that I have the power to do it."

But Flavia shook her head. "Nay, nay," she said, "what share can I have in it? I am but a poor helpless woman."

"And it is by performing womanly duties—ruling thine household with diligence and discretion—that I can now refund what is needful, and undertake this work for God, instead of continuing in the service of the emperor," answered Flaminius.

"Thou wilt write to the emperor concerning this matter?" asked his wife.

"I have already prepared a letter to send by the hand of a trusty messenger to Marcus Aurelius, so that I shall feel free to help these prisoners at once; after which I will travel to Ephesus and dispose of the slaves there, and if the persecution has ceased we may return thither to live; but it will not be wise for thee or Sisidona to go with me until we discover whether it is safe."

The news that the Roman stranger would undertake the cause of those who had been seized and
thrown into prison was eagerly welcomed by the
oppressed Church of Thyatira, and on the day appointed for their reappearance before the prefect
Flaminius stood forth as their counsel or orator.
He was well-acquainted with the laws of Rome,
and knew that those referring to the Christians
could be twisted to mean anything the prefect
chose to infer from them; but he knew, likewise,
that this was not their original intent; and so,
when he stood up in the Forum of Thyatira, he
called the attention of the prefect and assembled
lawyers to the celebrated letter of Pliny, proconsul of Bithynia, to the Emperor Trajan, some sixty
years previously, and upon which the law of Trajan was founded. This he knew was attacking the
enemy in their stronghold, for it was under this
law that they were tried and condemned.

"Noble senators, and ye people of Thyatira, this
Pliny, who was devoted to the service of the gods,
and by no means favourable to the Christians,
caused strict inquiry to be made into their manner of life and worship, and declared to the Emperor Trajan there was nothing in the principles
or conduct of the followers of Christ worthy of
blame, with the exception of their dissent from the
public religion. That the great Trajan thought this
but a slight offense is proved by this edict, which

forbade that the Christians should be officiously sought for, and that they should be punished only for refusing to sacrifice to the gods when brought before the magistrates in the ordinary way. This law was, however, wrested from its purpose so often and so flagrantly that another edict was issued by the Emperor Hadrian, commanding that for the future no Christians should be put to death except such as had been legitimately accused and convicted of some sort of crime. This law was re-enacted by our late emperor, Antoninus Pius, and also by our noble Marcus Aurelius. Wherefore, ye see that in searching for and meddling with these people who are honest and of good report, ye yourselves are guilty of breaking the laws of Rome; and ye would force these your judges and governors into open revolt against the emperor by condemning those whom he has declared innocent of any crime worthy of punishment."

It was curious to note the varied effect of this address upon the different auditors in the Forum. To the law-loving and law-abiding Romans the fact of the whole proceeding being against the letter and spirit of their edicts, and against the direct wish of their emperor, who was to them the visible embodiment of law, and greatly beloved, made it a serious matter, and they were in favour of the instant release of the prisoners. Not so the multitude. Roman law was to them but the mere machinery by which they were governed, and if this

OFFICIOUSLY: *aggressively*
WRESTED: *forcibly taken*
AUDITORS: *listeners*

could be turned aside by clamour and riot they were willing to join in either, led as they were by the priests of the public worship and the Jews, who so deeply hated the Christians.

The prefect, therefore, had no easy task, for whatever might be his private feelings toward the prisoners, or his respect for the laws of Rome, which he sat there to dispense and elucidate, he dare not altogether disregard the voice of the people, and this was most unmistakably against the Christians, so that sentence was again deferred; the prefect hoping that the popular fury against them would die out shortly, when a light sentence would pacify their accusers, or they could be dismissed entirely. What to think of Flaminius, and the course he had adopted, was an equal puzzle; and he had no means of ascertaining, for Flaminius left the Forum as soon as he had intimated that he should again defer judgment, and he was a stranger to everyone in Thyatira.

There was one, however, in that mixed assemblage who recognized Flaminius; and shortly after reaching home one of his slaves came to him with the intelligence that a priestess or attendant of the sibyl Sambethe desired to speak with him in the vestibule.

Flavia turned pale with alarm when she heard the message delivered, and Flaminius himself wondered what business this messenger could have for his private ear. He followed the slave, however, and

ELUCIDATE: *make clear*
INTIMATED: *hinted*
SIBYL: *prophetess*

soon stood before the closely-enveloped priestess, who, on seeing him, moved aside the long robe which covered her from head to foot, disclosing the features of his wife's former slave Nerissa.

Flaminius started as he recognized her. "Nerissa, is it indeed thyself?" he exclaimed.

Her head dropped lower under Flaminius' earnest gaze. "I am what thou seest me," she said, evasively; "but, my noble master, I came not to speak of myself, but for my brother, who now lies in the prison of Smyrna, charged with being a Christian. This is his only crime, and thou, who didst plead today in the Forum for those charged with the same fault, wilt thou not plead for him when he shall again be brought before the prefect?"

"But I do not understand. Is it Plautius, the vine-dresser, of whom thou speakest? He is in Rome, is he not?" asked Flaminius.

"Nay, but he followed me to Smyrna, as I greatly fear too late to prevent my—my—" and Nerissa stopped and burst into tears.

"But, Nerissa, surely thou who hast tasted of the love of Christ cannot be the servant of an idol?" said Flaminius.

"Nay, but Sambethe is not an idol, but a sibyl, who practices magic in a temple outside the walls of the city," answered Nerissa, with still drooping head.

"And thou hast been sold a slave to this temple service?" asked Flaminius, with a touch of self-reproach, as he reflected how hastily and inconsiderately he had called in the Thessalian slave-dealer and sold her.

But Nerissa shook her head. "Nay, but I escaped from my master at Smyrna, and went thither of my free will," she said.

"Of thine own choice?" inquired Flaminius, in surprise.

"Yes; I heard of the wonderful miracles wrought in this temple by some fellow-slaves from Thessaly who were going thither, and I thought this must surely be where the Lord worked in greatest power, and where His glory would begin to manifest itself, and so I hastened thither."

"And thou hast found out thy mistake?" asked Flaminius.

"Oh, would that I had been less impatient for the Lord's appearing!" said Nerissa. "I might then be able to meet Him with joy, but now I must bear the dread sentence, 'Depart from Me, ye cursed;'"[1] and, overcome by the bitterness of her feelings, she hastily wrapped the mantle about her head and left the house without speaking another word.

Later in the day Flaminius made fuller inquiry about this temple of magic, and found that Nerissa's account of it was correct, only that the true Sambethe had been dead long since; but those interested in the deceptions she practiced pretended that her spirit had descended upon one of her followers, who was a woman of Thessaly, while

[1] Matthew 25:41

the true Sambethe was a Jewess or Chaldean by birth, who had once been a Christian, and who, even after her assumption of magical powers, had such influence over many in the Church of Thyatira that even the angel or bishop tolerated her, and was rebuked by the Lord in this message: "I have a few things against thee, because thou sufferest that woman Jezebel, which calleth herself a prophetess, to teach and to seduce My servants to commit fornication, and to eat things sacrificed unto idols. And I gave her space to repent,...and she repented not."[1]

---

[1] REVELATION 2:20-21

CHAPTER XVIII

SARDIS

THE state of public feeling in Thyatira was at this time so strongly against the Christians, that Flaminius soon decided to remove his family to the neighbouring city of Sardis. This, like Thyatira, was the center of manufacturing interests, but the speciality for which it had attained its worldwide fame was the rich purple and crimson dye, which was extracted from a small shellfish abundant in the river Pactolus, near which the city stood.

The fabulously rich king of Lydia, Crœsus, once lived here, and he might with reason boast of his riches, when gold dust was to be found in the river-sand close by; but even this did not bring the wealth to Sardis that the *murex* did, with its crimson dye. Sardian carpets were likewise of worldwide fame, and the Persian kings had exacted a tribute of these, on which to tread as they mounted their horses. All these sources of wealth had contributed to the greatness of the city, but the Chris-

MUREX: *a type of shellfish*

tian Church, unlike her sister of Thyatira, was not correspondingly rich in patience and good works. She had a name to live, but was dead. The wealth and luxury and ease by which the Church was surrounded, had betrayed these Christians into a softness and effeminacy not at all consonant with the character of those professing to be soldiers of the cross. The love and care of these riches in which they abounded choked the word of God, so that the message, "Be watchful, and strengthen the things which remain, that are ready to die,"[1] was very needful. Some had heeded this message, for the Lord Himself had declared, "Thou hast a few names even in Sardis which have not defiled their garments; and they shall walk with Me in white: for they are worthy."[2] The Church now was in a much more flourishing condition than it had been while John was in Patmos; and so long as it was presided over by its bishop, Melito, it was not likely to sink into such deadness again.

The news that an advocate had been found for their persecuted brethren of Thyatira soon reached Sardis, and when it was known that he purposed removing to the latter place, a warm welcome was tendered to him, both by Melito and his flock.

Flaminius fully appreciated the kindness thus shown him, and an intimate friendship soon sprung up between him and the bishop, whom he consulted soon after his arrival upon the best

[1] REVELATION 3:2   [2] REVELATION 3:4
EFFEMINACY: *weakness or girlishness*
CONSONANT: *consistent*

means to be adopted for rescuing Nerissa from her present mode of life, and also for assisting Plautius to regain his liberty.

Flavia had seen Nerissa, and the sight of her beloved mistress had so overcome her that if she could only be taken from the temple service she professed herself willing to do or suffer anything. Flavia would gladly have received her again and reinstated her as her personal attendant; but Flaminius had advised caution, and his wife knew and trusted him so fully now that she could not only wait herself, but advise Nerissa to be patient and wait for her deliverance until a fitting time should come.

It was hard, perhaps, for her to wait now, but she had brought so much misery upon herself by her former impatience, that she readily agreed to this; the more so that Flaminius had promised to write to the prefect of Smyrna concerning Plautius, and also to befriend Julia, who with her child was now living at Sardis. How Nerissa had discovered her sister she did not say; but it was clear Julia knew nothing of her, for when Flavia went to see her she burst into tears, saying she feared Nerissa was dead.

"Nay, nay, she is not dead; but she cannot come to thee yet," said Flavia, soothingly. "She bade me come and tell thee she was well, and that she had not forgotten Julia, or the happy hours spent in the cottage in Aricia."

The mention of these happy bygone days brought the tears again to Julia's eyes; but she choked them back, and asked eagerly, "Where is Nerissa, then? Does she know I am in Sardis?"

"Yes, she came to my Flaminius to beg that he would plead with the prefect of Smyrna on your husband's behalf, and she told me where I should find thee."

But Julia had not heard the latter part of the sentence; at the mention of her husband she was quite overcome, and for a few minutes Flavia could only shed tears of sympathy for her great sorrow. Anxious, however, to arouse her from this, she spoke of the efforts Flaminius was now making to secure his release: but for some minutes she could only rock herself backward and forward, murmuring through her sobs, "I shall never see my Plautius again; he has been in prison more than a year, and will not live, even if he is rescued now."

"Nay, nay; the Lord, who has helped and sustained thee, will help him," said the lady, in a cheerful tone.

But poor Julia only shook her head. "I have not been shut up in a noisome dungeon," she said. "I have had to work hard, it is true, but I have breathed the fresh pure air, and my little one has been with me; but Plautius—" and again came a burst of sobs.

"What made thee leave Smyrna and come to Sardis?" asked Flavia, anxious to turn the conversation.

NOISOME: *foul-smelling*

"I liked not to be chargeable to the Church longer than was necessary; and hearing that two other women whose friends had been imprisoned were coming to work at the looms of Sardis, I came with them, for I had learned the art of weaving in Rome," replied Julia.

"And thou canst gain enough by thy labour to keep thyself and thy child?" asked Flavia.

"Not quite. The Church still assists me somewhat, but I am thankful that I am not wholly chargeable, now that so many are in need." And Julia turned to fetch her boy, who had grown to be a stout, rosy little fellow, the picture of health and happiness, in spite of the sorrow by which he had been surrounded all his life.

Flavia made some inquiries about him, and after placing something in his hand, which she thought might be helpful to his mother, she took her departure, promising to see her again as soon as any news could be obtained concerning her husband.

Flaminius fulfilled his promise of applying to the prefect of Smyrna for his release, but it was some time before he could get a hearing for his petition. In the meantime, however, he succeeded in rescuing Nerissa from her equivocal position, and after a time she was allowed to return as Flavia's personal attendant. He likewise took his projected journey to Ephesus, and sold off his slaves, leaving his household at Sardis.

EQUIVOCAL: *uncertain*

The application of Flaminius for the vinedresser's release was acceded to at last; but when Plautius came out of prison it was all too evident that his days on earth were numbered. The sufferings and deprivations he had endured had left their impress in his pale, emaciated face, and bowed, shrunken form. Even his affectionate wife scarcely recognized him, and some friends almost doubted his identity. Work, except of the lightest kind, he could never do again, for the strength of his manhood had been worn out of him in prison, and it seemed doubtful whether he would survive many weeks. All that friendly care and wifely solicitude could do was done for him; and it seemed after a time that he was better.

Flaminius was anxious to do something for Plautius that should be of permanent service to him; and, as he seemed to crave for some occupation, he at length decided to take a small villa on the outskirts of the village midway between Sardis and Smyrna; and in the cultivation of the garden attached to this his countryman might find health, occupation, and profit combined—considerations that induced both Flavia and Sisidona to warmly enter into the plan, so that the early spring witnessed their removal from Sardis to this rural home, and Plautius and his wife with them.

Flaminius had been too long engaged in an active life to resign himself entirely to the quiet retirement in which he now lived, and he was

IMPRESS: *mark*
SOLICITUDE: *attentiveness*
APOLOGY: *formal defense*

making active exertions for the benefit of his fellow-Christians in the neighbourhood. By his advice, Melito, the bishop of Sardis, was now preparing an "Apology" for the Christians of Asia, to be presented to Marcus Aurelius himself, as Justin Martyr had done twenty years before, when Antoninus Pius wore the purple. This famous "Apology" of the learned Christian philosopher had been the means of staying a threatened persecution against the Christians, and Flaminius hoped that another plea of a similar character from this Christian bishop might put a stop to that now so actively spreading from city to city and province to province. He knew, however, that the times in which they were now living differed greatly from the peaceful, prosperous years that marked the reign of the late emperor. For, under Marcus Aurelius, one disaster followed so quickly upon the heels of another, that the sagacity of the emperor and his ablest advisers was taxed to the utmost to devise means to meet all these complicated disasters, each of which in turn was charged to the agency of the Christians by their enraged fellow-citizens; so that it was no easy matter to preserve order among the unreasoning multitude, and protect from all harm the objects of their hatred, when fire and sword, earthquakes and inundations, pestilence and famine, marched through the empire in grim procession. This had been the history of the whole six years of the emperor's

STAYING: *stopping*
SAGACITY: *wisdom*
PESTILENCE: *deadly disease*

reign, and these disasters had not come to an end yet, so that Flaminius might well hold but a trembling hope for the success of Melito's "Apology."

When this document was prepared, the question of a suitable messenger had to be discussed. If Melito was to go in person and lay his plea at the emperor's feet, he could not go alone; and few of his flock had either the time or means at their disposal to accompany him, and at length he begged Flaminius to take this post of escort.

The calends of May were again approaching, and Flaminius had begun to grow anxious about his letter, sent to the emperor some time before, begging to be released from his duties at Ephesus. There had been ample time for a reply to be sent ere this, but no reply had come; and Flaminius' time to return to the proconsulate, so long postponed, was fast approaching. To go back, however, after the step he had taken at Thyatira, as the advocate of the Christians, was impossible, and, therefore, he was not unwilling to go to Rome on his own account, as well as to accompany Melito.

To take the whole of his family with him, however, would not be advisable, and so he decided to leave the children under the care of Sisidona and Nerissa, with the few trusty slaves that now formed their household, while Flavia went with him to Rome. He was the more anxious to depart and to travel with all speed, when the news came that the proconsul under whom he had served had died rather suddenly, for he knew not what construction might be put upon his absence from duty at such a time, if his letter had failed to reach the emperor's hand. So Flavia was urged to make her preparations for the voyage with all speed, that they might be in time for the next vessel leaving the port of Smyrna.

There was a pleasant farewell meeting at the house of Polycarp before the travelers took their departure. The aged bishop was anxious to send some message of remembrance to his friends at Rome by Melito; and so the family of Flaminius, with Plautius and his wife, and Nerissa and Melito, with the deacons and presbyters of the Sardian Church, were gathered around the hoary-headed saint to hear his voice once more—some of them for the last time. Together Melito and Polycarp had sat at the feet of the "disciple whom Jesus loved,"[1] and each had imbibed the spirit of his Master and theirs; and now they were sitting together for the last time on earth, holding sweet converse for the benefit of Christ's suffering Church in Asia.

"Dearly beloved, who are about to encounter the perils of the great deep, gird up the loins of your minds, be patient, be joyful in God. To Him all things in heaven and on earth are subject. Him every spirit serves. And may the God and Father of our Lord Jesus Christ, and Jesus Christ Himself, who is the Son of God, and our everlasting High Priest, build ye up in faith and truth,

[1] JOHN 20:2
HOARY-HEADED: *gray- or white-haired*
IMBIBED: *drunk in, absorbed*

and in all meekness, patience, gentleness, long-suffering, and purity; and may He bestow on you a lot and portion among His saints, and on us with you."

This was the apostolic blessing bestowed upon the travelers and their friends by the aged Bishop of Smyrna. He then tenderly embraced his companion and friend, Melito, and promising Flaminius not to forget his household during his absence, Polycarp bade them each farewell, noticing especially the little Cassius, who had come with Sisidona to see his mother and father embark.

Flavia could hardly tear herself from the embraces of her children when the moment for parting came, and she took Cassius to her arms again and again, almost regretting now that she had consented to leave her treasures behind. Bitterly as she felt this parting, its agony would have been increased tenfold, if she could have known what would befall her darling in a few short weeks. But the future is mercifully hidden from our view, and so Flavia turned from her boy and joined her husband, who was already on his way to the vessel. Cassius bravely dashed the tears from his eyes, and, young as he was, turned to say a word of comfort to his little sister.

"Don't cry, Flaminia, it makes our mother cry," he said; "and everybody seems to forget that God will stay at home with us and go with the ship too. I should like to do that too, thou knowest, but we can't, and so we ought to be glad, that being God's will."

Flaminia tried to stop her tears, for they almost prevented her recognizing the figures of her mother and father, as they stood on the deck of the vessel waving their farewells to the little group of friends on the shore. For nearly an hour they stood watching the vessel as she passed along toward the open sea, Cassius waving his hand as long as anyone on the deck could be seen; and then, at Sisidona's bidding, he turned to go home once more. He had looked his last on the noble faces of both mother and father, until they met before the throne of God.

On their way home they overtook the aged Polycarp; and Cassius, leaving the rest, went to walk beside him, slipping his hand into that of the bishop, and looking up inquiringly into his face.

"What wouldst thou ask me, my child?" said the bishop, noticing his looks at length.

"Mother has gone away in a ship," he said; "who will tell me about 'God is love' now?"

Polycarp looked down into the earnest upturned face. "Thou knowest God is love, dear child! Then thou canst ask Him to teach thee more of it Himself," he said.

"But wilt not thou help Sisidona to teach me, while Mother is away?" asked the child.

"But Sisidona may not need my help," said the bishop, with a smile.

"Nay, but she will," said Cassius; "she is not so good as my mother; nobody in the world is so good as my mother; but, perhaps, if thou helped Sisidona, it might be nearly as nice as what my mother says."

"Well, dear child, I will try to teach thee as thy mother does," said the bishop, again smiling at the little fellow's earnestness; and on bidding them farewell he told Sisidona he should visit them shortly.

CHAPTER XIX

SEEKING BUT NOT FINDING

ONCE more we must ask our readers to accompany us to the palace of Marcus Aurelius. He is sitting in his private room; the "Apology" of Melito is lying before him, and that of Justin Martyr, pleading on behalf of the same people, is beside it. He has been considering the claims advanced by these Christians, and comparing them with the philosophy which he had studied and practiced all his life. More sad and sorrowful than ever is the grand, noble face; for, struggle and strive as he will, Marcus Aurelius feels that he is still far from perfection, that he is powerless to subdue sin in himself. Perhaps, if he could have examined and compared these "Apologies" more carefully with the works of his favourite authors, he would have been led by the Spirit of God to see that these despised people had found what he and they were dimly groping after—a light to shine upon their minds and dispel the mists of philosophy and the darkness of superstition. But the

philosophers by whom he was constantly surrounded represented to him that the worshipers
of Christ were an irrational, turbulent, and pernicious sect, who ought to be put down. They would
have kept this "Apology" of Melito out of his hands,
if they could, and, failing to do this, they took care
to whisper hints and innuendoes of shameless orgies which the Christians dignified by the name of
religious worship.

"Their pretended bravery in the face of death
is mere hardihood and stupid obstinacy, without
reason or common sense," whispered these philosophers.

The emperor sighed. "I would to the gods it
were otherwise!" he said. "To what an admirable
state must that soul have arrived which is prepared
for whatever may await her—to quit her earthly
abode, to be extinguished, to be dispersed, or to
remain. By prepared, I mean that her readiness
should be exercised by a calm, deliberate judgment, and not by the result of mere obstinacy, like
that of these Christians."

And this was all philosophy could give to one
of her most earnest and devoted disciples—one
whose whole life was a struggle after a nobler, purer state than this world could afford—"the soul to
be extinguished, to be dispersed!" Was it wonderful that he looked sad when, feeling bitter dissatisfaction with this life and all it could afford, there
was no hope for eternity, no looking forward to a

PERNICIOUS: *evil, dangerous*
INNUENDOES: *suggestive remarks*
WONDERFUL: *surprising*

heaven beyond the grave?

No, Marcus Aurelius, the greatest and noblest of the Roman emperors, was poorer than the youngest child in our Sunday school, for he knew nothing of Christ, the Hope of the world. His philosophy could give him no help here in subduing sin or bearing grief, and no hope that beyond this life there is another which has been wholly redeemed by the blood of Christ from all sins, temptation, and sorrow.

Melito's "Apology" was not laid aside and forgotten altogether, as the philosophers hoped it might be. These Christians were his subjects, reasoned the emperor, however obstinate they might be; and Melito had pleaded wisely that his most beloved and honoured predecessors had protected the Christians from the rabble mobs who clamoured for their destruction; and that only Nero and Domitian, whose memories were detested, ever issued edicts against them.

These arguments had more weight with him, perhaps, than anything else, for he was at a loss to know which to believe, the philosophers, who affirmed that the whole of Christianity was framed on a lie, or the Christians, who declared they only held the truth. This, however, would cut the gordian knot. His predecessors had protected these people, and yet held fast to the public worship and the study of philosophy, and he would do the same.

CUT THE GORDIAN KNOT: *solve the problem with one bold stroke; from a legend about Alexander the Great cutting a knot that was impossible to untie*

So Marcus Aurelius turned from the further study of the Christian letters, or "Apologies," deciding that an edict should be sent to Asia, with as little delay as possible, to stop the persecution against these oppressed people. The heart of Melito was rejoiced almost beyond expression, except in praises and thanksgiving to God, for this great mercy. The hearts of the Christians of Rome, too, were made glad; and a special meeting for prayer and praise was held in the Church of the Catacombs.

Flavia, the last time she wended her way through the gloomy, torch-lighted passages to the Church, had scarcely dared to hope that her husband would ever accompany her, and yet he had most eagerly welcomed the invitation to meet with the brethren to thank God for turning the heart of the emperor mercifully toward them. Perhaps he felt that he needed the interposition of God in his own behalf now, for, in spite of frequent applications, he had not been able to obtain an audience with the emperor yet.

The Church of Rome had increased in numbers during the time Flavia had been away; but Anicetus had not forgotten the brave yet quiet patrician lady who came so seldom to join with them in the outward form of worship, and yet was so brave and true in her allegiance to God, that no opposition could daunt her, and no persuasions tempt her to deny her Lord and Saviour.

Flaminius had often wondered whether the emperor had received the letter sent from Thyatira, or whether he had heard of his forsaking the public worship of the gods in some indirect way. This was the sole reason Flaminius could think of to account for Marcus Aurelius treating him in the way he did, and he knew not what to do, for he was growing anxious to return to Sardis now, not only to avoid his former friends and companions, who treated him as one out of favour, and therefore to be neglected or scorned, as the case might be, but he was anxious to take Flavia back; for she had grown unreasonably anxious about the children, he thought. How to resist her appeals he did not know, and yet to leave Rome without seeing the emperor now might be the cause of much misconstruction and after-inconvenience, if not of positive trouble.

Flaminius was thinking of this as he silently followed his guide through the galleries leading to the Church, and inwardly praying that the Divine Spirit would teach him what to do—what step to take next in this difficult, dangerous business: for, if the emperor had been mortally offended at his joining the Christians and retiring from his post, it might be dangerous not only for him but for them likewise.

The latter fear, however, was removed, when he recollected the purpose for which they were meeting together; and it encouraged him to hope that

MISCONSTRUCTION: *misinterpretation*

his own case might not be so desperate after all; and even as he thought this there suddenly came to his mind the idea, that he might place himself in the way of the emperor as he went to the Forum; and he at once decided to act upon this suggestion.

Without informing Flavia of his intention, he went out early the next morning and took his way toward the great golden milestone near which Marcus Aurelius would alight from his chariot to enter the Forum. There was always a crowd of clients waiting here; and it must have touched the patrician pride of Flaminius very keenly to be seen waiting near this throng. But the Christian triumphed over the patrician, and, to his great joy, Marcus Aurelius relieved him from his unpleasant position the moment he saw him. For the emperor had hardly entered the Forum, when one of the imperial lictors came up, saying that the emperor commanded his attendance upon him immediately. With a silent thanksgiving to God, Flaminius ascended the steps and entered the vast hall, where, in one of the basilicas, the emperor held his court of justice. Marcus Aurelius had not yet ascended the tribune, but stood near one of the columns waiting for Flaminius.

He did not look pleased or vexed, but only intensely astonished, as his late secretary came before him.

"I knew not that thou wert in Rome, Flaminius,"

BASILICAS: *large courtrooms*
TRIBUNE: *speaker's platform*

said the emperor, sternly, without a word of greeting to his former favourite.

For a minute Flaminius could only look into that noble face, with its searching glance, in blank amazement.

"I have been in Rome some weeks, and presented several petitions, praying the noble Marcus to grant me an audience," said Flaminius.

"I have not seen one," replied the emperor.

"I likewise sent a letter by the hand of one whom I deemed a trusty messenger, many months since," said Flaminius, quickly.

The emperor slowly shook his head. "Thou must be mistaken in all this, or thy messengers must have failed thee; for I have seen nought of thy missives. I heard that thou hadst left Ephesus and forsaken the gods of Rome, before the death of the proconsul, or just at that time."

Flaminius feared he had been thus misrepresented to the emperor, and immediately drew from his girdle the letters-patent of the proconsul, not merely granting leave of absence, but commanding him to go to Pergamos for his health's sake.

Marcus Aurelius took the letter, but did not read it.

"Attend me later, in my private chamber in the palace," he said; and the courtier philosophers in attendance upon him bit their lips in silent vexation, that all their efforts to keep Flaminius

MISSIVES: *letters*
LETTERS-PATENT: *letters of permission*

out of the way had so signally failed.

Perhaps these men felt that if their gentle, earnest-hearted emperor once came to hear all the truth about the doctrine of Christ, their philosophy would be forsaken, and men like Justin Martyr and Melito would succeed them in the imperial favour. For the gods of Rome they cared nothing, but they loved the riches and honour and glory of living in a palace, however much their master might despise these things.

Marcus Aurelius never suspected these men of thus trying to ruin Flaminius. They were philosophers, and philosophy would teach them, as it had taught him, to hate and abhor every false way. This was how the emperor reasoned and believed; for he thought it was the study of philosophy that had given him the desire after holiness and purity, and the hatred of everything false and cruel. He knew not that every good desire of his heart—every earnest effort he was enabled to make toward the conquest of evil in himself—was through the guidance and help of God's Holy Spirit: that God after whom he was feeling if haply he might find Him, and yet from whom he was at the same time turning his eyes, when he refused to listen to or study the truth of this Christianity which was causing him so much trouble just now.

Flaminius, who had tried philosophy, and knew what it was worth, had been thinking thus, as he walked homeward, and wondered whether he

SIGNALLY: *notably*

should be allowed to speak plainly to the emperor of the glorious truths he had himself learned. For his own encouragement, and for use in argument, if he should need it, he took out the parchment roll containing the address of the Apostle Paul, before the court of Areopagus, at Athens, as recorded by the physician-disciple Luke, in his account of the Acts of the Apostles, and read these words: "God that made the world and all things therein ... and hath made of one blood all nations of men for to dwell on the face of the earth, and hath determined the times before appointed, and the bounds of their habitation; that they should seek the Lord, if haply they might feel after Him, and find Him, though He be not far from every one of us."[1]

"Surely Marcus Aurelius is one of the truest and most earnest of these seekers after God," said Flaminius softly to himself; "but will he recognize that what he is in search of has been revealed in Christ Jesus? If he will not submit his human philosophy to the claims of Christ, he may go on seeking; but he will go to the tomb without finding any other revelation, any other way by which he can be saved from the evil of this world and the darkness that hangs over the future. I will try to speak to him of this today; but will he listen? will he even hear my words?"

Flaminius might well sigh as he asked himself this question, remembering his own obstinacy on this very matter; and he could only pray that his

---

[1] ACTS 17:24,26-27

imperial master might be more open to conviction than he was. He took care to put his precious roll in his girdle before starting for the palace, and also to be there in good time to keep the appointment with the emperor. He was kept waiting long in the anteroom after his name had been announced; and he was glad to see when he entered that the emperor was alone.

"Now, Flaminius, state thy reason for leaving Ephesus for so long a season," said the emperor, quickly, as soon as the ceremony of entrance was over.

"There were two reasons, most noble Marcus," answered Flaminius; "my failing health and my wife's adherence to the Christian faith."

"What about thine own?" demanded the emperor.

"When I left Ephesus I believed as fully in the public gods as when I dwelt here at Rome. It was in Pergamos, in the very temple of Esculapius that my faith in these as divinities was shattered;" and he went on to describe the two nights spent in the sacred temple of healing, and the advice given to him by the flamens and physicians.

The emperor looked puzzled: "Thou hast been over hasty, Flaminius, in adopting thy wife's detestable creed; thou shouldst have had more wisdom than to listen to her specious arguments; for women are ever foolish in these matters."

"Many are, doubtless, most noble Marcus, but not my Flavia; she—"

SPECIOUS: *deceptively pleasing*

"Nay, nay, prate not to me of thy wife," said the emperor, testily; "but tell me, as though thou wert still my private secretary, is this sect well-nigh crushed out of Asia?"

"Nay, it will never be crushed out anywhere," answered Flaminius; "and persecution doth but strengthen its growth."

"Art thou speaking now as Flaminius the Christian, or as Flaminius the patrician?" asked Marcus Aurelius.

"As both," answered Flaminius. "I have seen the effect of fines, stripes, imprisonment, and death upon these people, as their persecutor; and I have learned the secret of their endurance, hope, and joy, since in their Scriptures—" and as he spoke Flaminius drew from his girdle the roll of parchment, and would have presented it to the emperor.

But Marcus Aurelius turned aside his head. "Of a weak and womanish character must thou be, Flaminius, to be thus easily turned aside from the study of philosophy," he said, scornfully.

The crimson colour rushed to the cheek of the proud patrician. "Nay, but I hold it as brave and honourable, instead of weak and womanish, to embrace this persecuted cause."

"Because it is persecuted? Then thou gloriest in casting thy lot among these people? Thy glorying shall soon be at an end. Statius Quadratus is the new proconsul; and he will receive my edict shortly to stop all proceedings against these people, and

PRATE: *babble*

let them sink to their original nothingness."

"Most noble Marcus, the Christians will everywhere render thanksgivings to God mingled with prayers on thy behalf for this great mercy."

"I want not their prayers; I know not their God or thine. As a Christian, thou knowest thou canst hold no office under the state, Flaminius," added the emperor, thinking this might move him. Flaminius bowed his head in acquiescence.

"I would ask a favour, but not for myself," he ventured to say, after a pause.

"Prefer thy request," said the emperor, shortly. Again Flaminius held forth the precious roll.

"If thou wouldst study this book, thou wouldst find what thou hast so long been seeking—what no other can reveal," he said, gently.

But Marcus Aurelius turned away. "I know not thy God," he said; "I shall hold my belief in philosophy and the gods of Rome until I die."

And he did. Truly these things are "hid from the wise and prudent;" but God has "revealed them unto babes."[1]

---

[1] MATTHEW 11:25

ACQUIESCENCE: *silent agreement*

CHAPTER XX

THE BURSTING OF THE STORM

THE aged Bishop of Smyrna kept his promise to Sisidona and the little Cassius, and more than one visit was paid to the small household, when not only Cassius, but the slaves, and Plautius and his wife, came to hear the words of wisdom and instruction that fell from the old man's lips.

The temporary improvement in Plautius was passing away, and it was easy to see he would not be with them long; but he moved about as actively as he could among the vines and orange-trees, for he was anxious that the garden should look its best when Flaminius returned, which would be early in the summer, or rather just after the first vintage had been gathered.

Everybody in Smyrna was making active preparation this year for a splendid celebration of their vine-god's festival, for the new proconsul, who usually resided at Ephesus, had promised to be present at some of the games; and the Jews and the priests of Dionysus had each determined to ask for more energetic steps to be taken against the Christians. Germanicus was still in prison, and they decided to ask, or rather to demand, that he should be given to the beasts in the arena.

The Church, hearing of this active enmity, once more grew alarmed for their aged bishop, and they besought him to retire from the city until after the storm had passed. But the great feast of Easter was near, and the old man was especially unwilling to be absent from his flock at that time. "And could ye rob me of my promised crown?" he added.

"Nay, but the Church needs thee still, my father," said one.

"Then, if it is so, the Lord will be a wall of fire about me, to defend me from the enemy," said Polycarp, firmly.

But some of them had received a hint that, if they wished to keep their aged bishop, he should be taken to a place of safety for a time; and they were determined he should go. "The Lord bade His disciples when they were persecuted in one city to flee to another; and we now come with this command from the Church, and bid you hasten to prepare for this removal."

"But whither shall I go?" asked Polycarp.

"To Sardis. Some of the friends of Melito will be sure to hide thee there."

But the bishop shook his head. "That will be the first place where they will seek for me, and I shall bring trouble upon those I would fain defend from it. Nay, if I must go, I will leave Smyrna quietly, and take refuge in the house of friends who are almost unknown to our city, with whom I may, peradventure, abide in safety."

Sisidona was soon communicated with upon the subject, and gladly welcomed the hoary-headed saint to their household; while Cassius was delighted at the change, having little idea why it was necessary, for Sisidona did not like to cloud the brightness of his young days by telling him that the religion they professed might at any time bring them into trouble.

Meanwhile events were slowly tending toward the destruction of the whole Christian Church of Smyrna. At least that was what the priests of the temples and the Jews intended, and their first victim was Plautius's friend, Germanicus. All the fashionable world of Smyrna had assembled in the arena to witness the games and do honour to this visit of the proconsul, who had ordered that Germanicus should be brought forward and sacrificed to the gods, or be cast to the beasts.

When Statius Quadratus saw the young man steadily refuse to do honour to Rhea or any of the idols, he begged him to have pity on his youth, and yield to this slight demand; but Germanicus made no answer, and the beasts were loosed upon him almost immediately.

PERADVENTURE: *perhaps*

The sight of this one victim so bravely enduring the agonies of death did but increase the popular fury, however; and the mangled remains of Germanicus were still being growled over by the hungry beasts when a cry was raised: "Away with all these atheists! Seek for Polycarp." And the proconsul, who had never heard the bishop's name before, ordered him to be brought before his tribunal the next day. But Polycarp's house was deserted, and many of those known to be Christians had left the city; and it was not until after a long search and many fruitless inquiries, that someone was discovered who had seen the old man go in the direction of the village where Plautius the vinedresser lived. So a party of soldiers was sent with Herodes, one of the magistrates of the city, to arrest the old man.

It was necessary, however, to find him first, and this did not prove an easy matter. One after another declared that neither Polycarp nor Plautius lived in that village, and the soldiers grew tired and ill-tempered over their bootless errand. At length a little boy was seen playing near the gate of a large garden, and one of the soldiers beckoned him to come to him. Without the least fear the child came, and the man led him aside to a copse near the road.

"Dost thou know any of the people called Christians about here?" asked the man.

"Yes," answered the boy; "I am a Christian."

BOOTLESS: *useless, unprofitable*

"Oh, thou art! art thou, my fine youngster? then we shall have thee, perhaps, to feed the beasts someday."

A faint colour came into the child's cheeks. "My name is Cassius," he said. "Wilt thou let me go now?" for he suddenly remembered that his father had bidden him before he went away never to talk to any stranger he might meet; and Sisidona had repeated this charge only a few hours previously. And he burst into tears as he thought of this.

"So thou dost want to run away, my fine fellow! Well, thou shalt go as soon as thou hast answered my questions. Thou knowest Polycarp, the wicked old bishop?"

Cassius's eyes flashed indignantly, but he would not answer.

"Now I know thou canst tell me all about this old man," said the soldier, giving him a shake; "so I mean to make thee. Dost thou understand?"

Still Cassius did not answer, although he was trembling in every limb.

"Dost thou hear? I will take thee off and give thee to the lion;" and this time the man struck him brutally.

But although smarting with pain, the brave little fellow still kept his lips tightly closed.

"Tell me where Polycarp is hiding, thou young traitor!" and this time the words were accompanied by a kick. The boy cried out with the pain, but he made no reply to this demand. Again and again was the question repeated with oaths and threats and cruel blows, until at length the boy could not rise, but lay on the ground a mass of bruises and bleeding wounds, while still the brutal coward kept beating him.

At length, however, he was compelled to cease, for the child had either fainted or was dead. And he turned away with an oath to join his companions, when another child unfortunately fell in his way.

With a blow and an oath he asked him the question he had little Cassius; and he dragged him under the trees, and pointed to his prostrate form.

"There, I will serve thee the same if thou dost not show me where old Polycarp is hiding."

The boy trembled with horror and apprehension as he gazed at the bleeding, prostrate form. "I will show thee," he said; and he led the way to the pretty villa where Sisidona was even then watching at the lattice for Cassius to come in.

The man released his hand as he silently looked at the house. "Thou canst go now," he said, "but don't let me see thee again." Hereupon the child ran away; and the soldier informed his companions of the discovery he had made, which was received with every demonstration of joy.

The captain of the band ordered them to surround the house, to prevent the possibility of escape, while the magistrate went to secure the prisoner.

APPREHENSION: *fear of what might happen to him*

Meanwhile Sisidona had grown anxious when the slaves came and told her that Cassius was not in the garden, and she was just issuing orders for a regular search to be made for him, when one of the slaves with a frightened face informed her the house was surrounded by soldiers. At the same time the magistrate appeared in the vestibule, demanding that Polycarp should be given up at once.

On hearing the demand Sisidona stepped forward, and, drawing herself up to her full height, demanded by what authority he entered her house unbidden, in the absence of its master.

"I come to arrest Polycarp, and the whole nest of Christians who shelter the evil old bird," answered the man, insolently.

"I do not question thy right to arrest me," said Sisidona, "for I am a Christian, but thou hast no right to enter this house to search for every fugitive from Smyrna."

She hoped by detaining the man for a few minutes Polycarp would escape or conceal himself; but as soon as the old man heard what had happened he came forward and gave himself up.

"The will of the Lord be done," he said; and turning to Sisidona he begged that food might be set before his captors.

While this meal was being eaten, the bishop retired to his own room and spent the time in prayer; but Sisidona could think of nothing but

INSOLENTLY: *rudely, disrespectfully*

the mysterious disappearance of Cassius. She had almost forgotten that she too was a prisoner, and would be carried off to Smyrna shortly, until the captain of the guard bade her get what she wanted to take with her to prison, as they would start at day-dawn.

A cold chill crept over her at that word "prison." She, the proud, gently-nurtured Roman maiden, shrank at the thought of this, and from contact with the rude, rough soldiers now feasting in the *atrium*. But worse even than this was the having to leave home at such a time; especially as she had no knowledge of what had become of Cassius. It was well she did not know, or her sufferings would have been even greater than they were; whereas now she could hope that the child would speedily return home. All night had the household been up in a state of alarm and agitation at the presence of the soldiers, who, after they had feasted, lay down to rest before starting on their journey again. At sunrise, however, they were all aroused, and Polycarp was summoned; for the captain had determined to reach Smyrna with his prisoners before the heat of the day.

The white-haired, noble-looking bishop was seated on an ass and rode first, while Sisidona was carried in a close litter guarded by soldiers. She would not be taken before the proconsul at once, she heard; for Polycarp only had been ordered to appear. And so she was thrust into prison for that

day, while the aged bishop went forward to confront his enemies alone.

It was the last day of the games, and the people were growing impatient at the long delay. The
proconsul's tribunal had been set in the stadium,
or amphitheater, that thousands might witness
his trial—if trial it could be called, where a prisoner's fate was virtually decided before his case was
heard.

At last the grand, noble old man was led in by the
band of ruffianly soldiers, and a great shout was
raised, as though some victory had been gained.
The painted and perfumed ladies in their upper
seats rustled their gay dresses and shook their
fans; the merchants, who had left their business
to witness the trial of this disturber of the public
peace, smiled; but the most bitter of his enemies
were the Jews, who were not slow in showing their
satisfaction at the proceedings.

Perhaps the persons most disturbed in that vast
assemblage were the proconsul himself and his assessor, who sat beside him. They had never seen
Polycarp before, and were struck with the serene
majesty of the old saint, as he stood on the sand-
strewn arena before them. Statius entreated him
to regard his great age. "Swear by the genius of
Cæsar, and I will release thee when thou hast re-
nounced thy Christ," said the proconsul.

Polycarp raised his head and looked round
upon that great multitude. "Eighty and six years

GENIUS: *guardian spirit*

have I served Him," said the old man, "nor hath He ever done me any wrong. Why, then, should I renounce my King and Saviour?"

"At least," said Statius, "swear by the genius of the emperor."

But Polycarp slowly shook his head. "Hear my confession," he said; "I am a Christian; and if thou wouldst know what that meaneth, appoint me a day and I will show thee."

"Knowest thou that I have beasts to which I will cast thee if thou dost not yield?" said the proconsul, angrily.

The old man's bright face grew brighter at this threat, and his upright form seemed to rise into greater dignity. Seventy years had he been bishop in this city of Smyrna, and no one in all that multitude could charge him with unfaithfulness or self-seeking; and now that his course was almost run, the message sent by the mouth of his master and teacher, John, was about to be fulfilled: "Be thou faithful unto death, and I will give thee a crown of life."[1] That crown was almost within view now; and above the angry shouts of the multitude sounded the words of His promise, "I will give thee a crown of life."

The proconsul, finding Polycarp was not to be either coaxed or frightened into denying his Lord, sent round a herald to proclaim, "Polycarp has confessed himself a Christian!" when the amphitheater rang with the cries of the exasperated multitude. "The teacher of Asia!" shouted some.

---

[1] REVELATION 2:10

"The father of Christians!" shrieked the Jews. "The enemy of the gods!" cried the merchants. "Away with him—with him who forbids us to worship!" exclaimed the women. And then, at last, came the dreadful, ominous roar, "Polycarp to the lions! The beasts for Polycarp!"

It was, however, the last day of the games, and the Asiarch who had control of the sacred games refused to break the rules at the cry of the mob. But they, not to be turned from their purpose of shedding the old man's blood, at once instantly called, "Bring fire for Polycarp!" and many rushed from their seats—the Jews being particularly forward in this—to bring in fagots to make the necessary pile. They rushed to the nearest baths and shops for these, so that it was not long before the pile was ready. Polycarp stood in his serene majesty, his eyes raised towards heaven, and his face beaming with joy, until all the hideous preparations were complete. Then he loosed his girdle and took off his sandals; and his hands being tied behind him, he mounted the pile, and the fagots were lighted.

Every shout and cry had subsided now, and that dense crowd could only watch with speechless pleasure the smoke as it slowly curled up toward heaven. But the silence was almost immediately broken by the voice of the martyr, as he burst forth into the thanksgiving he had so often used in the church close by: "Lord God Almighty, Father of our Lord Jesus Christ, Thy blessed and beloved Son, through whom we have received the grace

ASIARCH: *the Roman ruler of the province of Asia*
FAGOTS: *bundles of sticks or branches*

of knowing Thee; God of angels and heavenly powers; God of all things created, and of the just who live in Thy presence, I bless Thee for having brought me to this hour, that I may be among Thy martyrs, and drink of the cup of my Lord Jesus Christ, to rise to eternal life in the incorruption of the Holy Ghost. Receive me this day into Thy presence together with them, being found in Thy sight as a fair and acceptable sacrifice, prepared for Thyself; so that Thou mayest accomplish what Thou, O true and faithful God, hast foreshown. Wherefore I praise Thee for all Thy mercies. I bless Thee, I glorify Thee, through the eternal High Priest Jesus Christ, Thy beloved Son, with whom, to Thyself and the Holy Ghost, be glory both now and forever. Amen."

The flames had arisen from the light fagots of sweet-smelling wood, but they had been blown aside by the breeze, and so had not touched the aged martyr yet. The crowd were getting impatient now, for it seemed that the very elements were unwilling to injure him; and they angrily called for one of the attendants of the arena to kill the old man at once. A short sword was therefore plunged into his side; and the proconsul ordered the body to be burned. Then fashionable Smyrna went home to discuss what had happened; and after dark a few Christians crept to the arena and collected some of the martyr's bones, and buried them on the hillside, in the rosy dawn of Easter-day—a sad Easter to many hearts in Smyrna.

THE MARTYRDOM OF POLYCARP

CHAPTER XXI

AN UNEXPECTED MEETING

S ISIDONA was in such a whirl of perplexity concerning little Cassius, that she scarcely realized the danger of her own position, until she found herself in the dungeon at Smyrna; and then it was too late to devise any means for her own or her little nephew's assistance, even if she could have thought of anything.

The idea of being brought before the tribune of the proconsul alone, without a friend to speak a word for her, was alarming enough; and Sisidona shrank from the publicity this would involve with a nervous horror that was almost overpowering. She might escape this disgrace, she was told, by sacrificing to the gods at once; but she positively refused, and so she was led to where Statius Quadratus sat in state, at the upper end of the Forum.

The proconsul looked annoyed when he heard the charge brought against her. The murder of Polycarp had been quite enough, he thought, and he turned to speak to his assessor upon the subject; but the words were arrested on his lips by the look of anguish and horror in the young man's face.

He looked in vain among the crowd for the cause of this, until his eye fell upon the prisoner; then he saw that her face was white, and scarcely less agitated, while her eyes were fixed upon the young nobleman at his side in a widely opened stare, that seemed to betoken unconsciousness rather than recognition. The crowd, however, did not seem to have noticed his strange looks, and Sisidona's could easily be accounted for by her peculiar position. The proconsul saw this at once.

"Thy prisoner has been frightened by some tale of yesterday's tragedy," he said, speaking to the captain of the guard. "Take her back to prison," he added, "and bring her again tomorrow; she will then be better able to answer the charges brought against her."

The crowd murmured a little against this, but they were obliged to submit, and Sisidona was taken back to prison, hardly conscious of where she was going until she got there. As soon, however, as she was left alone, she seemed to realize more fully than ever her trying position, and a dreadful fear that she would deny her Lord took possession of her mind.

"I can never stand against this temptation; my heart is too weak and treacherous. I shall disgrace

BETOKEN: *be a sign of*

the holy name by which I am called. Oh, my God and Father, take this cup from me, or I shall perish!" she pleaded, in her agony of soul.

Gradually, however, she grew more calm. The words of comfort spoken to Paul years before came to her mind with power, as applied by the Holy Spirit: "My grace is sufficient for thee: for My strength is made perfect in weakness."[1] At last Sisidona could rest upon this, and feel that the battle she knew must be fought was not hers, but the Lord's, and He would strengthen her for all before her. The conflict began sooner than she expected; for a few hours afterward the door of the prison opened, and by the dim light that shone through the embrasure in the solid stone wall she recognized the young patrician.

In a moment she forgot everything but that he stood before her, and with a low cry she rose and tottered toward him.

He held out his arms and caught her, or she would have fallen to the ground. "Oh, Sisidona, that I should find thee thus!" he gasped.

"Claudius, Claudius!" was all she could utter; and then she burst into a violent flood of tears.

As soon as she had somewhat recovered, Claudius asked her how long she had been in prison, the particular charge against her, and where Flaminius was?

The first and last questions were easy enough to answer; but beyond the general charge of being

[1] II CORINTHIANS 12:9

EMBRASURE: *narrow window*

a Christian she knew not of what she was to be accused.

"Well, the matter can be very easily made right, if thou art not too obstinate. The proconsul has agreed that if thou wilt sacrifice to the gods tomorrow, thou shalt be at once released;" and then there followed a few whispered words that brought the rosy colour to Sisidona's pale cheeks.

But the next minute she had withdrawn herself from his protecting arm. "No, no, Claudius! I can never be thy wife," she said, "any more than I can sacrifice to the gods!"

"Nay, nay; but thou shalt follow this new superstition, if thou wilt only go to the temple sometimes. Nay, Sisidona, I came into Asia on purpose to find thee and tell thee this—tell thee I am sorry for my harshness and hastiness. Wilt thou not forgive me, my Sisidona?" he pleaded.

"If I had aught to forgive I would; but, Claudius, thou wast ever gentle and patient with me. It is I who need forgiveness of thee, but—but—"

"Nay, nay; say no more. We will not talk of this again—not until Flaminius comes back from Rome; but say thou wilt scatter a handful of myrrh on the sacred tripod tomorrow, and I shall be the happiest man in Smyrna."

But Sisidona shook her head. "I dare not—cannot deny the Lord who bought me," she said.

"We will not ask thee to denounce thy Christ—only worship the gods of Smyrna."

"Which would be denying the Lord of heaven. Listen, Claudius, and let me tell thee of that sad, dark time, when I seemed to be left a friendless orphan, alone in the world." She then went on to speak of her illness, and that time of sorrow in Ephesus when she first found the sweetness of the love of Christ.

He was quite willing to listen as long as she liked to talk, if only she would at the end comply with his request. At length he asked, "Dost thou know what will be the consequence of thy refusal to obey the proconsul?"

A slight shudder shook the young lady's frame. "They will throw me to the beasts, I suppose," she said.

He looked at her in astonishment. "Hath death no more horror for thee than that?" he said.

"Nay; I do not fear death, for Christ hath conquered it, and given us the victory, too. The pains of death will soon be over, and there is an eternal weight of glory beyond. Oh, Claudius, if I could only see and know that thou wert seeking this Saviour, and to be made a partaker of this glory, I would gladly walk forth to the beasts at once," she said, with clasped hands and glowing face.

For a few minutes he could only look at her in silent wonder; but at length he managed to say, "Sisidona, thou speakest of the glory beyond the arena for thyself, but what remains for me if thou art taken away?"

"Thou wilt seek to follow me, even as I have tried to follow Christ; only thou wilt be a better, braver Christian than I could ever be," said Sisidona, gently.

"What! embrace this Christianity after it has robbed me of all I hold dear? Never, Sisidona! it is impossible."

"Nay, nay; say not so; for I have prayed to God for this very thing, and to Him all things are possible."

But Claudius only shook his head. "I shall pray to the gods to break thy obstinacy," he said; "and then, if thou dost sacrifice to the gods once, thou mayest be released; and we will return to Rome, where no one will dare to interfere, even if thou dost go to that miserable Church in the Catacombs I have heard about."

To go to the despised Christian Church seemed the height of human folly to Claudius now. Would he always think the same? Would the name of Jesus always be despised and hated? Sisidona asked herself this question again and again after he left her, for it seemed that he hated the truth more and more, since it had brought her into trouble.

She had time to think of this, among other things, during the hours of the day and night, as they again slowly dragged themselves along. How often she had longed to see Claudius once more, to tell him what a mistake they had all made in supposing this Christianity was an unholy and impure faith; how she had yearned to tell him of the love of Christ, that had satisfied even her heart, with its multiplied wants and aspirations. And now he had come she did not feel that she could speak a word. She had tried to explain something of this, it is true, but her words had been poor and uninteresting, she thought—not at all as though she deemed it of the importance she did; and, thoroughly dissatisfied with herself, Sisidona could only pray that Claudius might be enlightened by some other means, since it seemed impossible that she could do her duty in this matter.

Just before the daylight had quite faded the jailer brought her a letter. The waxen tablets were bound together by a silken cord, and tied in the fashion Claudius always adopted. With trembling fingers she untied this, and read the few words written within:

Claudius to Sisidona, greeting. The proconsul hath determined to conduct thy trial in private, so that the submission required of thee will be slight—only sufficient to warrant the sending forth a herald to proclaim that thou hast sacrificed to the gods. Thou wilt therefore hold thyself in readiness to perform this slight service, and return home, for the sake of—

CLAUDIUS

Sisidona sat and gazed at the waxen tablets long after the fading daylight had prevented all recognition of the beloved characters engraved upon them, while a fierce struggle went on in her breast. Should she yield to this temptation? It seemed sometimes that she must; but at length came the word of promise again, "My strength is sufficient for thee." With this to rest upon, she was at length able to sleep, and she did not awake until summoned to go to the proconsul next morning.

He received her graciously—even kindly, and warned her with great tenderness against the danger of learning to follow obstinate atheists, like Polycarp, whose life had been taken for his misdeeds.

It was the first time Sisidona had heard the fate of the gentle bishop, and she visibly started as it was mentioned now. The proconsul followed up the advantage he thought he had gained by ordering the spices to be brought at once, that Sisidona might scatter them on the sacred fire. But they held them in vain toward her.

"I cannot forsake the Lord my God by burning incense to demons," said Sisidona.

"Renounce thy Christ then, and thou shalt be released," said the proconsul; and Claudius looked at her with a white, pleading face, that was harder to resist than the persuasions of the proconsul. But to both Sisidona could only give what seemed a hard, unfeeling denial; and when she had done this she covered her face with her hands, and groaned in the agony of her spirit.

After a short consultation she was ordered to be taken back to prison, and in a few hours Claudius visited her again. Every temptation that could be thought of was placed before her to induce her to yield, but without effect, until at last she said, "Oh, Claudius, do not tempt me further, and do not ask me to explain my faith again. I cannot talk worthily of the great theme, but I can die for it."

"Nay, nay; Sisidona, I must see thee as often as possible; but I promise not to ask thee to forsake thy religion again. Is there anything I can do for thee? no message I can take to thy friends?"

"Yes, indeed, if thou wilt, I should be glad to know whether Cassius has been found, and how Plautius and the household are faring during my absence;" and having directed Claudius how to find the house, she requested him to wait a few minutes, while she wrote some messages to be delivered to Julia, the wife of Plautius, who would hand them to their proper owners.

She then took her tablets, and upon some of them wrote, or rather drew, the figures of two fishes. Upon others she drew a circle, with a cross in the center, and the first and last letters of the Greek alphabet, while Claudius sat and watched her.

"Why art thou doing this?" he asked at length.

"It may be my last message to these friends," she said, "and I would fain assure them that I die in the faith of Christ, and likewise would give them something whereby their own faith may be strengthened. No one understands these signs but Christians; therefore we can send messages in this way without fear of discovery by our enemies."

"But thou wilt explain them to me, my Sisidona," said Claudius, anxiously.

She looked doubtful as to the wisdom of doing this, but his next words assured her she might safely trust him. "These signs shall be as sacred to me as to thee, Sisidona," he said; "as sacred as thou thyself art to me. These fishes, what will they tell to thy fellow Christians?"

"This is the message they will carry, 'Jesus Christ, God's Son, the Saviour,' because the initial letters of these words form the Greek word for fish," answered the lady.

"And this with the circle and the cross?" asked Claudius.

"The circle represents eternity, and the cross inside shows that Christ by dying upon the cross saveth to all eternity," she said.

"And the Greek letters Alpha and Omega?"

"Jesus Christ, the first and the last, the beginning and the end. The persecutions have compelled Christians to adopt signs in writing, or they could never send messages to each other without discovery, when discovery would be dangerous."

"No one shall discover these or see them, until I place them in the hands of this vinedresser's wife," said Claudius, as he took them; and with a sad farewell he took his departure, and went at once in search of Flaminius' house.

The slaves, he found, were like a frightened flock of sheep; but by degrees he made them understand that, although he came from Smyrna, it was on a friendly errand, and at once asked for the children, and where they had found little Cassius.

"We found him, indeed, noble Claudius, but it was only to bring him home to die," said one of the slaves, dashing the tears from his eyes as he spoke.

"Was he ill then, or had he met with an accident?" asked Claudius, in alarm.

"He had been beaten—beaten to death, because he would not betray our good bishop, Polycarp. Another boy of the village has told us all about it since;" and the slave fairly broke down at the recollection of that tale of horror.

The slaves led Claudius to the little white-draped chamber where the body of the murdered boy lay; and Claudius himself broke down, Roman as he was, at the sight of that fair young form all cut and gashed and disfigured with bruises. The household were at a loss to know what to do with the body, for every relative was away, and Claudius could only suggest that he should be laid in a temporary grave in the coolest part of the garden, until his father returned, when it could be burned with the customary honours.

246 OUT OF THE MOUTH OF THE LION

Claudius then asked for Julia, and was directed to a small cottage standing in a corner of the garden. Plautius, he was told, had been ill ever since the arrest of Polycarp and Sisidona, and so he was not surprised to see Julia in tears, as she opened the door. That he had just left Sisidona, and brought a written message from her, was quite enough, however, to secure him a welcome; and so he was soon standing by the dying bed, for Plautius was slowly dying, not of any disease to which a name could be given, but from the effects of that long imprisonment that had sapped the springs of his life.

"Plautius, here is a message from the noble Sisidona, who is still in prison," said his wife, leaning over him as he lay.

He slowly opened his eyes and looked at her. "Tell me she has not denied her Lord," he whispered, feebly.

"Look," said Julia, and she held one of the tablets before him and read its translation.

"She will die for her faith," said Claudius, sadly.

"The Lord be praised! The love of Christ is worth a thousand lives, if we had them all to give," said Plautius, with astonishing energy. It was his last effort—the last words he spoke. He uttered a faint moan a few minutes afterward, and then his ransomed spirit took its flight to that land where there is no dying.

CHAPTER XXII

CONCLUSION

CLAUDIUS RUFUS was pacing up and down in the *atrium* of the proconsul's house at Smyrna, impatiently waiting for an audience, and brooding the while over no very pleasant thoughts, as it seemed; for his brows were knit and his fist clenched involuntarily, as he passed up and down.

In a few minutes the slave drew the curtain at the farther end of the hall, and admitted him to the *peristyle*, where the proconsul met him and asked eagerly, "Hast thou succeeded, Claudius?"

"I never shall induce her to give up her faith," he said.

The proconsul looked vexed. "Then nothing can save her from the beasts at the next games. Has she heard of the death of these Christians?" he asked.

"Yes; and I have told her now of the ruffians beating little Cassius to death, for she questioned me so closely concerning the child that I could not keep it from her any longer. I wish Flaminius had returned from Rome," added Claudius, with a sigh.

"I wish he had, and would leave this Christianity behind him," said the proconsul. "Why men can't leave it alone, when they see it brings nothing but trouble, I cannot tell. If it were not for this Christianity Flaminius might now have been the proconsul of Asia, for he stood high in the emperor's favour, I know."

"Thou hast no reason to complain, then, of Flaminius, since thou hast succeeded to what should have been his seat," said Claudius.

"Most true; but it does not make the folly of thy friend the less. Look at him—he has had to forfeit the favour of Marcus Aurelius, see all his plans for advancement cut off, sink into obscurity, when he might have commanded the highest honours in Asia; and tarnish the honourable name of his ancestors by being called Christian; and for what does he barter all this? What does he gain by it?"

The question of the proconsul beat its refrain through the mind of Claudius until he could think of nothing else. What was to be gained, to be achieved by this new faith, that seemed to be turning the world upside down? Certainly Flaminius had not been given to wild-brained enthusiasm about anything, unless it was in his devotion to the emperor, until this Christianity seized him; and as for Sisidona, it seemed at one time that nothing could stem the current of her pride, ambition, and extravagance. Her hair had glittered with the abundance of the gold-dust in its coils, more brilliantly than any other Roman maiden in Faustina's court; and now it seemed that she had not only given up the use of this, but could make herself happier within the bare prison walls than she was in the palace, surrounded by every pomp and luxury that she could desire, or that could gratify the most exacting taste. And what was the gain for all this loss? for gain there must be, or Sisidona would not have been singing, as she was the last time he went to her, and looking as happy as she had often looked restless in those old days of pomp and splendour.

This question puzzled Claudius more than he cared to own even to himself; and before the day was over he found himself at the prison once more, not to torture Sisidona with persuasions to forsake her Lord and Master, but to ask in a humble, teachable spirit what the secret of this new faith could be.

Sisidona was not wholly unprepared for this, for Claudius had asked many questions lately that had indicated a growing interest in this matter; but, mistrusting her own ability to impart this wonderful news of salvation, she lent him her precious parchment roll, containing the Gospel of John, which he took home with him and promised to study carefully.

POMP: *showy display*

And thus some weeks slipped away; the proconsul vainly hoping that the outcry against the Christians would grow less fierce, and Sisidona praying that Claudius might, if it were possible, be spared the pain of seeing her suffer. He had ceased to urge her to sacrifice to the gods, for he himself had given up the worship of these dumb idols. At heart, indeed, he was already a Christian, but he hesitated to avow it, fearing that it was love for Sisidona rather than a higher and purer motive which actuated him. She, too, counseled caution and delay. Ready to brave death herself without shrinking, she begged him not to rush headlong into needless perils by a premature and uncalled-for declaration of his infant faith, but to await the guidance of his Master in the matter, lest in the moment of trial his courage and confidence should fail.

Sisidona, too, was anxious that he should avoid rushing into danger, at least until the arrival of Flaminius and Flavia, that he might break to them the tidings of little Cassius' cruel death as gently as might be, for the slaves would have little discretion in doing this, she knew, and the news would be heavy enough and sorrowful enough, however it might be lightened in the telling. So Claudius promised to watch the arrival of every vessel from Rome, to meet his old friend at the harbour; and, that he might not be absent at this time, he begged the proconsul to appoint a deputy in his place

ACTUATED: *motivated*

when he returned to Ephesus.

Statius looked uneasy. "I know not that a deputy can be obtained, Claudius," he said; and then added, "Thou wilt be better away from Smyrna at this time."

"Better away from Smyrna?" repeated Claudius; and then he was seized as with an ague.

"Dost thou mean that—that Sisidona is to suffer?" he asked, in a low, hoarse whisper.

"I have been obliged to yield to the demands of these clamorous Jewish merchants," answered the proconsul, turning away as if to avoid the discussion of an unpleasant subject.

But Claudius arrested him with another question before he had left the *atrium*. "One other word," he said; "does she know this?"

"I gave orders that she should hold herself in readiness for the forthcoming games in honour of Rhea," answered the proconsul.

"It is well. We will both be in readiness," said Claudius, with forced calmness.

"Will both be in readiness?" repeated the proconsul. "Thou dost not mean that thou wilt throw thy life away for this obstinate damsel?"

"Nay, I shall not throw my life away, but give it for the truth I have learned from Sisidona's lips; for I too am a Christian."

"Say thou art a madman, and it will be nearer the truth!" answered the proconsul; but Claudius did not hear these words, for he had rushed from

AGUE: *fit of chills and shaking*

the house, and was on his way to the prison. He was going to comfort Sisidona, as he said, but it was rather to receive than to give comfort, for at the sight of her calm composure all his strength and courage failed him, and for a few minutes he could only bow his head and weep bitter tears of agony.

"Sisidona, thou must grant me my last request," he managed to say at last. "I believe in Christ as my Saviour, and I will die with thee for His truth."

But Sisidona shook her head. "Nay," she said; "but thou must live for the truth; thou art not called to die for it yet."

"But thou must die, my Sisidona;" and he shuddered as he spoke.

She bowed her head. "God can make dying easier than living."

"The pains of death at least will be short, and I cannot live without thee," said Claudius.

"Thus thou wouldst die for me—commit self-murder, and call it dying for the truth. Nay, nay, my Claudius, it must not be. God will give thee grace to live, even as He gives me strength to die; for I have sometimes trembled at the thought of death, even since I have known that the sting is taken away."

"And thou art not afraid now?" asked Claudius.

"Afraid!" said Sisidona. "Thinkest thou I should be afraid to travel to Rome to meet thee? And this death is but a shorter journey, and the dear Friend waiting to welcome me is Christ Himself. I often wished I could conquer the fear of death, Claudius, but I see now that God does not give us dying grace to live with, for we do not need it; and so, as He supplies me with just the strength I need to die, He will give thee all that thou needest to live."

In vain Claudius pleaded that many had given themselves up to die for the truth, and that the steadfastness of the martyrs encouraged others to persevere. Sisidona would not yield even a reluctant consent to this self-immolation, and at length Claudius was obliged to promise that he would not accuse himself, or do anything rashly, but patiently abide by the advice of Flaminius and Flavia, whatever that might be.

The day for the citizens of Smyrna to assemble in the amphitheater once more came—all too soon for Claudius. Flaminius had not arrived, but a vessel from Rome was expected almost hourly, and Claudius had begged in vain that the games might be postponed until its arrival. The proconsul smiled, as he might at the whim of a frantic child, and asked what good it would do? whereas it might cause a riot to put off the festival of the goddess. This was too true, as Claudius knew well enough, and yet, like a drowning man, ready to catch at a straw, he cheated himself with the hope that if Flaminius could only reach the city in time he might save Sisidona yet.

SELF-IMMOLATION: *voluntary sacrifice of himself*

He was, indeed, like a frantic child, until that last visit to Sisidona—not in the prison where she had hitherto been confined, but in a small cell under the arena, and within sound of the yells and roars of the savage beasts and more savage men.

"I am glad thou hast come, Claudius," she said, taking his hand as he entered. "I want thee to give me up—give me up to God; that is what He asks thee to do for Him now," she added.

"Sisidona, it is too much; I cannot do it. If it was my life now—if I could take thy place I could bear it, but to give thee to such a death!" and he covered his face with his hands, but bravely stifled his emotion.

"And yet, my Claudius, God has done more for thee. Think of it. He gave up His only Son to the slow agony of thirty years' living with sinners, and then had to shroud His omnipotence, and see Him die an excruciating death for the sake of those who were crying, 'Crucify Him, crucify Him!' Thinkest thou that Christ cannot sympathize with thee in this sorrow, when He, too, had to bear the separation from His Father, that was keener pain than the thorns or nails could inflict? My Claudius, think of all He endured for thy salvation, and then from thy love to Him thou wilt be able to give me up."

Together they kneeled on the damp, cold floor, but it was Sisidona who pleaded with God for this grace for Claudius—grace for him to live submissively to God's will. For her sister and Flaminius she prayed too; and then, as she rose from her knees, she begged that Claudius would go at once to the harbour, and await the coming of the vessel, lest her sister should hear too abruptly of her own death.

At first Claudius was unwilling to do this, but Sisidona appeared greatly disturbed at his refusal. "I cannot tell thee why I wish it so much, my Claudius," she said; "but of this I am sure, a great calamity will be prevented if thou dost reach the vessel as soon as possible."

"Then I will go, my Sisidona; and the Lord be with thee until my return, for I shall certainly see thee again," he added.

Sisidona shook her head as the door closed behind him, and then, fearing lest the sounds from the arena should daunt her, she gave herself up to prayer, not only for herself, but for those whose lives would be shadowed to the grave by a great sorrow, that God would help and teach them how to live. Meanwhile, Claudius had mounted his chariot, and driven at the top of his speed away from the sights and sounds of the festive games. A party of wrestlers were entering the street leading to the amphitheater, looking eager and expectant, and he thought with horror that when their contest was over, and the leafy crown placed on the victor's brow, his beloved Sisidona would be in the cruel grasp of the lion, and the sand that they would trample and scatter in their mock conflict would be dabbled and stained with her blood. The thought was agonizing, and he lashed his horses into a more furious gallop, and kept them at this pace until the harbour was reached, and he was obliged to alight. Giving them into the charge of his slave, he went to inquire for the imperial galley that was expected to make the port shortly.

The vessel was here already, he was told, outside the harbour waiting for the breeze to spring up and bring her in. Weary of nothing so much as inaction, and anxious to discover whether Flaminius was on board, he drew out a handful of sesterces and offered them to the first boatman he saw, to row him to the galley. The man needed no second bidding for such a reward, and a few minutes afterward he was shouting to the shipmaster, demanding to know the news in the name of the proconsul.

On hearing this, a herald stepped forward bearing the imperial arms and holding up a formidable-looking packet. "I am the bearer of an edict from Marcus Aurelius, tribune of the people and emperor, to Statius Quadratus, proconsul of Asia," he said

"What is this edict?" asked Claudius.

"To stop the persecution of the Christians," said another voice; and Melito, the Bishop of Sardis, looked over the side.

But Claudius did not heed who the speaker

might be. "Get down into this boat and come with me, if thou wouldst deliver the message of the emperor ere it be too late!" he said. "They are even now in the amphitheater, and we may not be in time." And at that thought huge drops of perspiration bedewed his brow, as he helped the herald to descend.

To row to the shore and jump into his chariot, which was still waiting, was the work of a very few minutes. He neither saw nor heard Flaminius and Flavia calling to him; he was deaf to everything; oblivious to everything but that life and death rested in the hand of the man he was bearing to the amphitheater—and they might be too late even now.

Heedless of every impediment, Claudius urged his horses to their utmost speed, and kept them at it. Quiet citizens sitting in their little canvas booths in the street might call to him to draw rein, or his chariot would be dashed to pieces and the horses killed. What did he care for horses or chariots with Sisidona's life at stake? On he dashed, until the private door of the amphitheater, leading to the proconsul's box, was reached. His official dignity secured his entrance here, and as the door closed behind him a dull roar, that seemed to shake the very building, betokened that there was some change in the sports; and Claudius grew white with horror, as he thought it might be Sisidona brought to confront the

IMPEDIMENT: *obstacle*

lion.

Bidding the herald keep close behind him, he rushed along the narrow passage and mounted the stairs close at the proconsul's elbow, while right before him stood Sisidona.

Sick, faint, giddy, he almost reeled at the sight, while the proconsul asked, "Wilt thou sacrifice to the gods even now?"

"Hold!" thundered Claudius, before Sisidona could reply, and he thrust forward the messenger of the emperor, who instantly handed the huge parchment, with its ponderous seals, to the proconsul.

"Citizens of Smyrna, ye see with what haste this messenger hath come from Rome, to bring this word of command from your emperor; it is meet, therefore, that ye should now hear what this word is." And he proceeded to read the imperial edict commanding that the Christians should remain unmolested within the province until further orders were received under the seal of the emperor.

To describe the effect these words had upon that vast assemblage would be impossible. Like wolves cheated of their prey, they uttered one long, low growl when they saw Sisidona taken back to her cell unhurt; but beyond this they dared not go.

Claudius could hardly wait to answer the questions of the proconsul in his haste to reach Sisidona once more, for he knew that this sudden rescue would overcome her more even than her impend-

PONDEROUS: *massive*
MEET: *appropriate*

ing danger had done, and he was likewise anxious to ascertain whether Flaminius and Flavia were on board the imperial galley.

The latter question was answered more speedily than he expected, for Flaminius presented himself at the door of Sisidona's cell shortly after he himself had arrived. Over that meeting we will draw a veil, for there were tidings of the deepest sorrow as well as the holiest joy to be imparted; for, while Sisidona had been snatched from the jaws of death, and they could rejoice with thanksgiving for this, the family circle was not complete, and Flaminius and Flavia would sorely miss the welcome of their lovely, noble boy, whose baby brow was wreathed with the martyr's crown in the heavenly kingdom. The loss of Polycarp and their humble friend Plautius likewise added to their weight of sorrow; and at length they decided to leave Asia and return to Aricia, taking the widowed Julia with them.

Nerissa accompanied her sister, for she had proved beyond question that her departure from the simplicity of the truth as it is in Jesus had been deeply and truly repented of, and the widow clung to her in her sorrow more closely than ever, so that not only Flavia, but Flaminius himself, promised to help her in assisting her sister to gain a livelihood at the work of weaving, and likewise to recommend her for re-admission into the Christian Church—a privilege she had forfeited by joining in the service of Sambethe. In this particular,

Sisidona's word of recommendation would be as law to the Church, for having barely escaped martyrdom, she had secured the privilege—so often abused afterward—of recommending those who had lapsed or fallen away to be received again, on her giving them a testimonial of fraternal love. This she readily gave Nerissa, and so there would be little difficulty in gaining re-admission to the Church at Rome, and the poor girl grew more hopeful and cheerful as the time for their departure drew near.

As Christians, all public offices were closed to Flaminius and Claudius; but to be able to live in peace and retirement was an unspeakable mercy, and this was granted to them, for no active persecution against the Christians was permitted in Rome during the remainder of the reign of Marcus Aurelius; although in other parts of the empire there were frequent outbreaks of popular fury against these oppressed people. But in each of these, as they arose, the Christians proved themselves faithful and true—loyal unto death—loyal unto the end.

"And what shall I more say? for the time would fail me to tell of [those], who through faith subdued kingdoms, wrought righteousness, obtained promises, stopped the mouths of lions, quenched the violence of fire, escaped the edge of the sword, out of weakness were made strong, waxed valiant in fight, turned to flight the armies of the aliens?

FRATERNAL: *brotherly*

Women received their dead raised to life again: and others were tortured, not accepting deliverance; that they might obtain a better resurrection: and others had trial of cruel mockings and scourgings, yea, moreover of bonds and imprisonment: they were stoned, they were sawn asunder, were tempted, were slain with the sword: they wandered about in sheepskins and goatskins; being destitute, afflicted, tormented; (of whom the world was not worthy:) they wandered in deserts, and in mountains, and in dens and caves of the earth. And these all, having obtained a good report through faith, received not the promise: God having provided some better thing for us, that they without us should not be made perfect. Wherefore seeing we also are compassed about with so great a cloud of witnesses, let us lay aside every weight, and the sin which doth so easily beset us, and let us run with patience the race that is set before us, looking unto Jesus the author and finisher of our faith."[1]

THE END

---

[1] HEBREWS 11:32-12:2

ABOUT THE AUTHOR

Emma Leslie (1837-1909), whose actual name was Emma Dixon, lived in Lewisham, Kent, in the south of England. She was a prolific Victorian children's author who wrote over 100 books. Emma Leslie's first book, *The Two Orphans*, was published in 1863 and her books remained in print for years after her death. She is buried at the St. Mary's Parish Church, in Pwllcrochan, Pembroke, South Wales.

Emma Leslie brought a strong Christian emphasis into her writing and many of her books were published by the Religious Tract Society. Her extensive historical fiction works covered many important periods in church history. Her writing also included a short booklet on the life of Queen Victoria published in the 50th year of the Queen's reign.

Emma Leslie Church History Series

GLAUCIA THE GREEK SLAVE
A Tale of Athens in the First Century
After the death of her father, Glaucia is sold to a wealthy Roman family to pay his debts. She tries hard to adjust to her new life but longs to find a God who can love even a slave. Meanwhile, her brother, Laon, struggles to find her and to earn enough money to buy her freedom. But what is the mystery that surrounds their mother's disappearance years earlier and will they ever be able to read the message in the parchments she left for them?

THE CAPTIVES
Or, Escape from the Druid Council
The Druid priests are as cold and cruel as the forest spirits they claim to represent, and Guntra, the chief of her tribe of Britons, must make a desperate deal with them to protect those she loves. Unaware of Guntra's struggles, Jugurtha, her son, longs to drive the hated Roman conquerors from the land. When he encounters the Christian Centurion, Marcinius, Jugurtha mocks the idea of a God of love and kindness, but there comes a day when he is in need of love and kindness for himself and his beloved little sister. Will he allow Marcinius to help him? And will the gospel of Jesus Christ ever penetrate the brutal religion of the proud Britons?

SOWING BESIDE ALL WATERS
A Tale of the World in the Church
There is newfound freedom from persecution for Christians under the emperor, Constantine, but newfound troubles as well. Errors and pagan ways are creeping into the Church, while many of the most devoted Christians are withdrawing from the world into the desert as hermits and nuns. Quadratus, one of the emperor's special guards, is concerned over these developments, even in his own family. Then a riot sweeps through the city and Quadratus' home is ransacked. When he regains consciousness, he finds that his sister, Placidia, is gone. Where is she? And can the Church handle the new freedom, and remain faithful?

www.SalemRidgePress.com

EMMA LESLIE CHURCH HISTORY SERIES

FROM BONDAGE TO FREEDOM
A Tale of the Times of Mohammed
At a Syrian market two Christian women are sold as slaves. One of the slaves ends up in Rome where Bishop Gregory is teaching his new doctrine of "purgatory" and the need for Christians to finish paying for their own sins. The other slave travels with her new master, Mohammed, back to Arabia, where Mohammed eventually declares himself to be the prophet of God. In Rome and Arabia, the two women and countless others fall into the bondage of man-made religions—will they learn at last to find true freedom in the Lord Jesus Christ alone?

THE MARTYR'S VICTORY
A Story of Danish England
Knowing full well they may die in the attempt, a small band of monks sets out to convert the savage Danes who have laid waste to the surrounding countryside year after year. The monks' faith is sorely tested as they face opposition from the angry Priest of Odin as well as doubts, sickness and starvation, but their leader, Osric, is unwavering in his attempts to share the "White Christ" with those who reject Him. Then the monks discover a young Christian woman who has escaped being sacrificed to the Danish gods—can she help reach those who had enslaved her and tried to kill her?

GYTHA'S MESSAGE
A Tale of Saxon England
Having discovered God's love for her, Gytha, a young slave, longs to escape the violence and cruelty of the world and devote herself to learning more about this God of love. Instead she lives in a Saxon household that despises the name of Christ. Her simple faith and devoted service bring hope and purpose to those around her, especially during the dark days when England is defeated by William the Conqueror. Through all of her trials, can Gytha learn to trust that God often has greater work for us to do *in* the world than *out* of it?

www.SalemRidgePress.com

Additional Titles Available From

Salem Ridge Press

YUSSUF THE GUIDE
*Being the Strange Story of the Travels in Asia Minor of
Burne the Lawyer, Preston the Professor, and
Lawrence the Sick*
by George Manville Fenn
Illustrated by John Schönberg
Young Lawrence, an invalid, convinces his guardians, Preston the Professor and Burne the Lawyer, to take him along on an archaeological expedition to Turkey. Before they set out, they engage Yussuf as their guide. Through the months that follow, the friends travel deeper and deeper into the remote regions of central Turkey on their trusty horses in search of ancient ruins. Yussuf proves his worth time and time again as they face dangers from a murderous ship captain, poisonous snakes, sheer precipices, bands of robbers and more. Memorable characters, humor and adventure abound in this exciting story!

MARIE'S HOME
Or, A Glimpse of the Past
by Caroline Austin
Illustrated by Gordon Browne R. I.
Eleven-year-old Marie Hamilton and her family travel to France at the invitation of Louis XVI, just before the start of the French Revolution. There they encounter the tremendous disparity between the proud French Nobility and the oppressed and starving French people. When an enraged mob storms the palace of Versailles, Marie and her family are rescued from grave danger by a strange twist of events, but Marie's story of courage, self-sacrifice and true nobility is not yet over! Honor, duty, compassion and forgiveness are all portrayed in this uplifting story.

www.SalemRidgePress.com

For Younger Readers

DOWN THE SNOW STAIRS
Or, From Goodnight to Goodmorning
by Alice Corkran
Illustrated by Gordon Browne R. I.
On Christmas Eve, eight-year-old Kitty cannot sleep, knowing that her beloved little brother is critically ill due to her own disobedience. Traveling in a dream to Naughty Children Land, she meets many strange people, including Daddy Coax and Lady Love. Kitty longs to return to the Path of Obedience but can she resist the many temptations she faces? Will she find her way home in time for Christmas? An imaginative and delightful read-aloud for the whole family!

SOLDIER FRITZ
A Story of the Reformation
by Emma Leslie
Illustrated by C. A. Ferrier
Young Fritz wants to follow in the footsteps of Martin Luther and be a soldier for the Lord, so he chooses a Bible from the peddler's pack as his birthday gift. When his father, the Count, goes off to war, however, Fritz and his mother and little sister are forced to flee into the forest to escape being thrown in prison for their new faith. Disguising themselves as commoners, they must trust the Lord as they wait and hope for the Count to rescue them. But how will he ever be able to find them?

AMERICAN TWINS OF THE REVOLUTION
Written and illustrated by Lucy Fitch Perkins
General Washington has no money to pay his discouraged troops and twins Sally and Roger are asked by their father, General Priestly, to help hide a shipment of gold which will be used to pay the American soldiers. Unfortunately, British spies have also learned about the gold and will stop at nothing to prevent it from reaching General Washington. Based on a true story, this is a thrilling episode from our nation's history!

www.SalemRidgePress.com

Historical Fiction by William W. Canfield

THE WHITE SENECA
Illustrated by G. A. Harker
Captured by the Senecas, fifteen-year-old Henry Cochrane
grows to love the Indian ways and becomes Dundiswa—the White
Seneca. When Henry is captured by an enemy tribe, however, he
must make a desperate attempt to escape from them and rescue
fellow captive, Constance Leonard. He will need all the skills he
has learned from the Indians, as well as great courage and determination, if he is to succeed. But what will happen to the young
woman if they do reach safety? And will he ever be able to return
to his own people?

AT SENECA CASTLE
Illustrated by G. A. Harker
In this sequel to *The White Seneca*, Henry Cochrane, now eight-
een, faces many perils as he serves as a scout for the Continental
Army. General Washington is determined to do whatever it takes
to stop the constant Indian attacks on the settlers and yet Henry
is torn between his love for the Senecas and his loyalty to his own
people. As the Army advances across New York State, Henry re-
ceives permission to travel ahead and warn his Indian friends of
the coming destruction. But will he reach them in time? And what
has happened to the beautiful Constance Leonard whom he had
been forced to leave in captivity a year earlier?

THE SIGN ABOVE THE DOOR
Young Prince Martiesen is ruler of the land of Goshen in Egypt,
where the Hebrews live. Eight plagues have already come upon
Egypt and now Martiesen has been forced by Pharaoh to further
increase the burden of the Hebrews. Martiesen, however, is in love
with the beautiful Hebrew maiden, Elisheba, whom he is forbidden
by Egyptian law to marry. As the nation despairs, the other nobles
turn to Martiesen for leadership, but before he can decide what to
do, Elisheba is kidnapped by the evil Peshala and terrifying darkness falls over the land. An exciting tale woven around the events
of the Exodus from the Egyptian perspective!

www.SalemRidgePress.com

CPSIA information can be obtained at www.ICGtesting.com
Printed in the USA
LVOW070737240313

325713LV00001B/11/A